WHISPER

A THRILLER

BRIAN DEARBORN

Copyright © 2023 by Brian Dearborn.

The right of Brian Dearborn to be identified as the author of this work has been asserted.

All rights reserved.

No part of this book may be reproduced, stored in a retrieval system, or transmitted, in any form, or by any means (electronic, mechanical, photocopying, recording or otherwise) without the prior written permission of the author, except in cases of brief quotations embodied in reviews or articles.

It may not be edited, amended, lent, resold, hired out, distributed or otherwise circulated, without the publisher's written permission.

This book is a work of fiction. Except in the case of historical fact, names, characters, places, and incidents either are products of the author's imagination or are used fictitiously. Any resemblance to actual persons, living or dead, events, or locales is entirely coincidental.

Published by Brian Dearborn.

ISBN: 979-8-9874701-1-4

Cover design: Michael Rehder / rehderandcompanie.com

Interior formatting: Mark Thomas / Coverness.com

*To my dad, Fred Dearborn, for his love of reading and collecting books.
I miss you every day.*

WESTPORT, CONNECTICUT

Friday, April 1, 2022
10 p.m.

S pring had never felt so dead.
The snow fell steadily in the darkness, a dry powder, soft and quiet. It lay over the firepit, hot tub, and thick clutches of trees bordering the property. Amy raised a finger to the sliding glass door and swept it back. Cold. Too cold for April. Where are the snowplows?

She drew the cashmere cardigan tight around her and turned to the couch with the warm fur blanket. She heard a howl and paused. A wolf. Or dog? Wolves were not common in Connecticut. Maybe in northern New England. She stepped quickly to the switch plate and turned on the backyard lights. Probably just the wind.

She opened *Sleeping with the Enemy* and set the bookmark down, sipping from a glass of Brunello on the side table. It had been a stressful week. The department was made up of mostly male accountants and insurance actuaries. She was the first female manager, as well as the youngest at just thirty-five. They weren't ready for the shift. Thank God for weekends. Relaxation, quietude, hot tub.

She looked around the living room; the white-painted brick fireplace, the built-in bookshelves with framed photographs showing a menagerie of family and friends. One photo, larger than the others, sat on the center shelf. Madison and her at the beach on a warm Fourth of July in Cape Cod. They had spent one week after high school graduation at Madison's family vacation home.

In the background of the photo was their friend Dawn asleep on her beach towel. Amy peered closer and saw Zane, Madison's older brother, walking out of the ocean. She laughed to herself, remembering the prank they had played on him later that day after finding out he had a crush on her. Amy hadn't wanted that trip to end. Madison was leaving to attend college out of state. She had feared they would slowly drift apart.

She sipped from the Brunello again, then peered over the back of the couch into the brightly lit backyard with the giant lazy flakes of snow, gleaming as they fell. She wiggled deeper into the fur blanket and smiled. So cold outside and so warm in here. *Home.*

The hot tub would be even warmer. She gulped the remaining wine in her glass and climbed the white staircase, holding onto the black banister, and into the master suite. In there was the walk-in closet she'd always wanted, every girl's dream; shelves lining each wall, filled with clothes from Christian Dior and Chanel. She opened a drawer in the center island, pulled out a black one-piece bathing suit, slipped out of her blue jeans, and pulled off the cashmere cardigan. She spotted the Google Nest Mini speaker in the closet.

"Hey Google, play Celine Dion's 'Where Does My Heart Beat Now.'" Her and Madison's favorite song growing up. They would often play it while getting ready together.

As she sang the dramatic melody in front of the full-length mirror, she studied her long, slender build and strawberry-blonde hair flowing down past her shoulder to the middle of her back. In high school, she'd always wanted long hair. Now, she hardly recognized herself. This woman was successful and beautiful, if she were to believe the reflection before her. So different from the shy, insecure woman in the photograph of her and Madison in Cape Cod. She ran a hand along her thigh. Sometimes, good things happened with hard work. She looked away from the woman in the mirror as the song ended, grabbed a white bathrobe, and walked back downstairs.

She grabbed the iPad on the kitchen island and touched a finger to the icon; one hundred and two degrees. The hot tub would be perfect in five minutes. As she waited, she turned on the flat-screen TV in the kitchen, eager for some background noise. The faint howling of the wind that permeated the house was almost too eerie. She reached for her cell phone, glancing through her notifications and messages.

Amy paused and typed a text message to Madison.

Hey friend—I miss you. I hope you're doing okay. When are you coming back home?

She hit send and turned over the phone. Why did Madison have to live in California now? So far away.

She blankly stared at the TV screen for several minutes until the hot tub reached the desired temperature. Then she walked to the sliding doors that led to the outdoor patio. Opening them slowly, she felt a frigid breeze rush inside. She sprinted toward the hot tub, quickly pulled off the cover, and jumped in. The warm water provided a calming relief from the bitter air outside.

The snow was falling at a lighter pace now, and the lights from the house shone brightly against the night sky. She turned her body toward the woods, leaning her head back and gazing up, letting the snowflakes fall gently on her face. Embracing the sense of calm and stillness, Amy closed her eyes.

Following her breath, she counted each inhale and exhale. For a brief period, she drifted off to sleep. Meditation always seemed to put her mind at ease and helped her cope with the inevitable waves of anxiety. Slowly opening her eyes again, Amy looked out once more toward the woods before turning around to face the house.

Darkness. The house was only a faint outline in the black. But she had left the lights on in the kitchen, family room, upstairs bedroom, and outdoor patio. The light and jets in the hot tub were still on, so it wasn't a power outage. The iPad was inside, so she couldn't have accidentally turned them off while dozing. What was going on?

She reached for the towel, dried off, put on her bathrobe, and darted toward the sliding doors, rushing inside to escape the cold air. After locking the door behind her, she fumbled in the dark with a sliver of light from the front porch streaming through the main foyer. In the kitchen, she turned on the lights and located her phone.

But where was the iPad? She had definitely left it on the kitchen island.

The inside lights flickered off again. She stood motionless in the darkness, unsure of her next move until she heard a thud from the front of the house. She grabbed her phone, turned on the flashlight, and inched toward the main foyer and around the dark corner. The outside wind chilled her skin. The door was open. The wind picked up and pushed at the door. It swayed back and forth, hitting the wall. She stepped into the door frame and peered outside into the light snow, looking feverishly from side to side. Nothing out of the ordinary.

"Hello?"

Silence.

She slammed the front door shut and turned on the main foyer light.

As she was about to dial 9-1-1, her phone rang. Amy jumped and let out a gasp. It was her mother, Elizabeth, and she felt a sense of relief.

"Mom, I'm so glad you called."

"Hi, honey, you sound worried. Is everything okay?"

"Something strange is going on. The lights in the house have been going on and off. My iPad is missing. The front door slammed open—"

"The wind? Maybe you left it—"

"No. I know I locked it. I looked out front, but no one was there."

"Call the police. I'm jumping in the car."

"No, no. It's really bad out. It's not safe, and it'd take forever for you to get here. I'll be fine. I'll call the police now."

"Okay. Then call me back immediately. I love you, sweetie."

"Love you too." She hung up and as her index finger hovered over the nine, the phone rang. Unknown number.

"Hello—this is Amy Carlisle speaking."

No response.

"Hello?"

She hung up and just as she was about to dial 9-1-1 again, the phone rang again. Unknown.

"Hello!"

A robotic voice, neither male nor female, responded on the other end.

"Hi ma'am, sorry to bother you. Is Elizabeth there?"

"No, I'm sorry. Elizabeth doesn't live here. You have the wrong number. Bye now…"

"Before you go, may I ask you something?"

Amy leaned against the front foyer wall and took a breath. Maybe it was one of the teenagers on the street, bored and pranking her. "Sure, go ahead. What is it?"

"How has the storm been for you in Westport? It's crazy to think we're getting snow in April."

Amy peeked out the front window. "Yeah, it's calmed down a bit now though. Not snowing as hard as it was earlier. How do you know I live in Westport?" Must be the boy who lives on the corner. Little jerk.

"Your phone number. It's a Westport area code. Are you sure Elizabeth isn't there and that you're alone in the house?"

She ended the call. This was too much. Before she was able to dial 9-1-1, an alert appeared on her phone. New text message.

I know you are alone.

The sender was typing another text and she waited as the little dots floated on the screen, trying to slow her breathing.

For now.

The foyer light turned off and an object crashed through the window next to the front door. She screamed and crouched down, covering her head. It was the iPad which was now laying on the floor with broken glass.

Another text dinged.

Coming in!

Amy slowly looked up to the cracked window, with light from

the porch streaming through. All was still and quiet. The light was suddenly blocked by a shadowy figure who leapt through the window. Glass flew everywhere. The figure landed on Amy and she was flattened to the wood floor. She saw a large hunting knife in their hand. Long, black steel blade. Brown leather handle.

She struggled, punching and scratching but the figure pinned her down, straddling her chest, stomach, and arms beneath their legs. They grabbed hold of her neck and she gasped for breath as a gray faceless mask stared down at her. No mouth. Two black pits for eyes covered by a black filter. It was secured to their head by elastic straps.

Amy's bathrobe had fallen open and the figure's black suit slid over her skin. She imagined a giant python squeezing her neck. The knife rose, shimmering in the light.

She struggled and managed to loosen her right hand, frantically scurrying her fingers across the floor until she landed on a large piece of glass. She brought it up fast and hard, stabbing the figure in the left arm. She'd aimed for the neck.

Still, she was free. Her phone was nowhere to be seen, so she grabbed the iPad and ran for the stairway. Halfway up she stopped and turned to see the figure pull the piece of glass from their arm. They tilted their head from side to side. The expressionless mask was haunting.

The figure got to their feet, and Amy ran to the top of the stairs as they swiftly walked toward the staircase. She sprinted down the hall to the master bedroom and locked the door. A bookcase stood to the right. Adrenaline pumping, she pushed it in front of the door and paused, surprised there was no sound yet from the other side, before running to the closet.

There was no lock on the inside of the closet and she looked around for anything she could use to block the door but the shelves were attached to the wall and the center island was cemented to the floor.

She pushed aside her cocktail dresses to reveal a half-sized door to the attic. She pulled the dresses back over the doorway to disguise her location, climbed through and shut the door. She followed the narrow staircase inside to the upstairs attic, partially finished and filled with storage boxes. The space was largely empty. Not many places to hide. Toward the back, two large windows rested on either side of a door that opened onto a small third-story deck. She leaned against the doorway, still clutching the iPad in her hands, thankfully working but low on charge. She dialed 9-1-1.

A female voice on the other end answered.

"9-1-1, what's your emergency?"

"There's a masked intruder inside my house trying to kill me. Please send help." Her whisper was too soft, and she worried the woman couldn't hear her. It was hard to breathe.

"Ma'am, can you please verify your location?"

"125 West Grove Lane, Westport, Connecticut."

"Ma'am, are you in a safe space now away from the intruder?"

"Yes, I am hiding in the attic. The intruder is somewhere downstairs." She minimized the phone call on the iPad screen and pulled up the cameras on the home security system. She scrolled through each room. There was no sign of the intruder on the main level.

She then heard a loud thud below her.

Clicking on the master bedroom camera, she saw that the bookshelf she had used as a barricade had toppled over. She scrolled to the master closet and saw the creepy figure moving around. Suddenly, the person turned toward the camera and held up the knife. The faceless mask again sent a shiver down Amy's spine.

The figure stood for a few moments then moved toward the dresses hanging in the closet and pushed them to the side. They must see the door.

"They've found the door to the attic. I need to find a safer hiding place."

"Get to a safe space until police arrive. I know there is some bad weather in the area—it may take up to twenty minutes."

"Okay, please hurry."

"Ma'am, just stay on the line with me until help arrives."

"I will."

She needed to focus on hiding. There were no hiding places in the attic—everything was open and exposed. She opened the door to the third-floor deck. The only option was down.

Tripping over her bathrobe, she stepped outside, the snow stinging her bare toes. She closed the door behind her and glanced over the railing and immediately spotted a large snowbank that had accumulated on the main level, likely from snow that had slid off the roof.

She glanced back inside and saw the intruder enter the attic room.

With little time to think, she jumped over the railing and fell three stories down to the snowbank, the iPad slipping from her hands.

The light powdery snow mostly cushioned the impact, yet the cold stung her like a thousand knives. She searched feverously for the iPad upon landing, knowing the dispatcher was still on the line. She glanced up toward the deck and saw no sign of the attacker. They were likely inside, headed back downstairs and in her direction. She had no time to continue searching.

Amy hoisted herself up and eyed her surroundings. Inside wasn't an option, not even in this cold weather. The steam still rose from the hot tub. She raced over and jumped in, bathrobe on, and pulled the cover over her head. The cover allowed a few inches to breathe above the water line.

The water was warm and soothing and loosened the muscles in her legs and shoulders. She closed her eyes and forced herself to breathe slowly and listen hard. It would be at least ten more minutes for the police, now. She did her best to listen for footsteps or any sound but the bubbling water mostly drowned out any other noise.

She suddenly heard a subtle scratching on top of the hot tub cover and she placed a hand over her mouth, slowing her breath to a deathly silent pattern. She counted in her head. *Breathe in, Mississippi. Breathe out, Mississippi.* The scratching became louder, then disappeared completely. She sat anxiously in the warm, bubbling water. *Breathe in, Mississippi...*

A knife tore through the cover, slicing down an inch from her nose. She screamed in horror. The intruder retracted the knife and she quickly took a deep breath and descended beneath the water as the knife penetrated again. Looking up, she saw the tip of the black blade directly overhead. The blade was not quite long enough to touch the surface of the water.

The knife pierced the cover again. When she couldn't hold her breath any longer, she hesitantly broke the surface of the water, gasped for air then swam to the other side. In the distance, she was relieved to hear the faint sound of police sirens. The knife didn't appear again. Maybe the police scared them off. Amy quietly pushed up on the cover and peaked outside. No sign of anyone. The sirens were closer now. She waited a few more seconds then slowly stood up while gasping for air.

As the steam began to clear, the outline of the gray mask took form, and the knife raised, plunging into her chest. She fell back on the side of the hot tub, her lower body still in the hot water. She tried to fight back but the knife had pierced her deeply. She was losing blood and consciousness quickly.

She struggled for breath and taking one last glance above her, the figure paused, leaned over her, and whispered in her ear.

"You have Madison to thank."

She tried to murmur something back as she stared into the black eyes, but the blood began to pool in her mouth.

The knife, gleaming in the cold spring night, raised one last time and plunged through her heart.

The water turned crimson red as the jets gently rumbled on. The snowfall was picking up, and it turned red as it landed on Amy's motionless body.

1

Breaking up was never easy.

"I think you left a few button-ups in the closet." Madison watched as Kyle picked up the last of his belongings, still in a daze. Three years. Just months before this, she had settled on being with him forever, though she knew he wasn't her soul mate. She secretly dreaded the thought of becoming *Mrs. Sorrento*.

The first year was a typical honeymoon phase—great conversations lasting for hours, exciting adventures, exotic trips, and amazing sex. Something quickly changed in year two after they moved in together. Their differences unveiling, they became even more apparent in the third year. But the longer the relationship, the harder it was to leave. Was she making the right decision?

Get yourself together Madison Parker.

She reminded herself why she was doing this. Being in this relationship was making her lose her natural vivaciousness, and in the last year especially she had started to feel numb to it all. That numbness was eventually a wake-up call that something needed to change. In the past she had tried to talk with Kyle openly and honestly about how she was feeling, but she felt disregarded and unheard. If he wasn't working at his job as an ER nurse, he spent most of the day glued to his phone. Resentment started to build.

Madison saw last year's Christmas photo in the corner of the bedroom. Her and her rescue puppy Penelope, a Boston terrier, in front of the Christmas tree. Kyle was noticeably missing.

It was the first Christmas she had not been home to spend time with family and friends in Connecticut. Determined to make things work with Kyle, she had decided an intimate holiday together in San Diego would be the perfect way to rekindle their fading relationship.

Unfortunately, he ended up having to work over much of the Christmas break in the ER and they were barely able to spend any time together. Now, with it all over, Madison was more upset than ever that she'd sacrificed family and friend time at home to try and be with Kyle. Seeing the sad look in her eyes in the photo, masked by a slight smile, reminded her how lonely she had felt on that Christmas morning, something she vowed would never happen again.

Most regrettably, she missed one last Christmas with her dad who passed away weeks later.

Madison knew the only option was to end it; she had admiration for Kyle but craved more affection. She watched him pack. It was warm and sunny outside, a perfect San Diego April afternoon. Just a week ago they had been at the beach.

"If you find anything else, please let me know."

"I will." She paused. "This is really hard, Kyle. To say goodbye after all these years."

"I feel the same way. Maybe our paths will cross again, even if it is only as friends..." Saying *friends* stung him. He had said more than once that he was still very much *in love*.

Before walking out, he reached down to give Penelope a giant hug and kiss. Kyle and Penelope had grown close. This goodbye was just as hard for him as it was for her.

The door gently closed behind him and she stood in silence before slowly sliding to the floor and pushing her face into her hands. The ugly cry came hard and fast. It was the official end, the right path, yes, but happy memories were flooding back now. Like the time she opened the front door and Kyle was standing there drenched after a huge rainstorm, holding three dozen roses on Valentine's Day. The same door her back was now against.

Penelope gently licked her cheek.

"It's okay girl. I'm okay."

Penelope wouldn't have it and whined, licking at her cheek again. Her attention eventually calmed the tide. It was true. Everything would be okay. Eventually. She collected Penelope into her arms. "Okay. Enough of that." She wiped away the tears, stood, and walked through the hallway toward the kitchen. She stayed at the kitchen island for a few minutes, looking out the floor-to-ceiling windows. There were high-rise buildings to the left and an unobstructed bay view directly in front of her.

Living on the twentieth floor usually made her feel on top of the world, but right now it made her feel lonelier and more isolated than ever. As though she was far removed from earth, from reality.

She was beginning to sound like Kyle.

She grabbed a glass from the cabinet and poured some water from the refrigerator. She glanced down and saw Penelope was still at her side, gazing up as she tilted her head back and forth. She smiled as she reached for a dog treat in one of the cabinets.

On the counter was her work laptop, and she debated for a few moments whether she had the energy to open it. It was Saturday but work was starting to bleed into the weekends. She hesitantly turned on the computer, first scrolling to her Outlook account. There were already forty unread emails since last night.

Feeling agitated, she was pulled back into her job. She was an account manager for a large biotech company that developed and commercialized life-transforming medicines. The job seemed to consume her life at times. Lately, the department had become increasingly male-dominated and egocentric, lacking the heart and soul that once inspired her. Much like she was feeling in her relationship, she felt as though she was settling in her work life as well.

After responding to emails, she glanced down at the clock on her laptop. 4 p.m. That was enough for the day—she was ready to start her weekend. Slamming the laptop closed, she grabbed her phone and jumped on the couch as Penelope snuggled up in between her legs. She scrolled through social media. She stopped on a photo her older brother Zane had posted—a selfie of him wearing a suit in the airport. Probably another business trip.

She opened her text messages. Amy Carlisle had texted last night. It was nice to see a message from her hometown best friend. She hadn't seen her since January.

Hey friend—I miss you. I hope you're doing okay. When are you coming back home?

She was about to type a response when a new text message appeared from Jessica.

Hola chica, hope everything went okay today with Kyle. Break-

ups are never easy. Are you still able to make it out tonight? Bradley is coming too!*

Jessica Rodriguez was one of her best girl friends in San Diego. She owned a dance studio in Mission Beach called The Heat, and Madison had taken one of her classes after first moving to the city close to ten years ago. They'd remained close ever since.

Madison had also met Bradley Jackson at Jessica's studio. She'd recently helped him secure a position at her company as an account manager. Bradley, openly gay, was proud to refer to himself as Madison's "other" boyfriend. Both Bradley and Jessica brought out her wild side; the three of them used to party hard, before Kyle. Many weekend nights had spilled into the early-morning hours, a hazy blur of drinking, dancing, and after-hours parties.

That was all mostly behind them now, though, on rare occasions, they would relive their glory days.

Fresh off a break-up, tonight had the hallmarks of being one of those times. Armin van Buuren was in town, playing at one of the city's most infamous night clubs, known for its basement vibe, that specialized in house music. Madison had bought tickets a few months before breaking up with Kyle. Even then, she'd had a desperate feeling that she needed a night out with her friends, a chance to let loose and forget her worries.

Kyle had always made her feel guilty about socializing with friends. A wave of excitement and anticipation overtook knowing she wouldn't have to answer to anyone tonight. She responded immediately.

Hey Jess! Thanks for making me feel better. Been a tough day but getting through it. I am still up for tonight! Can't wait to see Bradley too. Meet at my place at 8:30 p.m. for some pre-drinks. See you soon!

The early-evening sun shone brightly through the windows and glistened on the bay outside as Madison drifted off into a deep sleep on the couch.

She awoke a few hours later to the mellow hum of her phone vibrating. The stars faintly shone against the crystal-clear sky outside. A gentle breeze from the open balcony door whipped at her feet as she reached over to grab her phone, realizing she had a few unread text messages. Before she had time to open and respond to them, she noticed the time.

8 p.m.

"Shit!" Madison exclaimed. She only had thirty minutes to get ready.

Madison poured herself a glass of prosecco for the shower. She picked out a newly purchased outfit—a fitted black cut-out dress that framed her thin, toned silhouette perfectly. After applying her makeup and fixing her shoulder-length, wavy blond hair, she added the final accessories to her outfit: a pair of gold hoop earrings, a bracelet, and pink peep-toe heels to add a pop of color.

She then reached for the necklace her dad had gifted her on the day he passed. The golden key pendant on the thin gold chain shimmered in the light as she put it on. She held the small key in her hands once it was around her neck. She felt a sense of comfort every time she touched it, as if Dad was giving her a warm embrace.

Back in the main living area, she dimmed the lights and pulled out a few long-stemmed champagne flutes from the cupboard. The doorbell rang, followed by an insistent knocking that caught her off guard. She could hear laughter from the hallway.

She opened the door slowly, and the laughter grew louder. She could distinctly hear Bradley's cheerful and expressive voice.

"Party's here!" Bradley and Jessica screamed, each waving a bottle of champagne in their hands. Madison let out a long laugh while embracing them with open arms.

She led them to the main living area, handing them each a glass of prosecco from the kitchen counter. She admired her friend's attire; Jessica was wearing a light pink cutout dress which contrasted nicely against her tanned skin and straight, long, brown hair. Bradley was dressed in all black, sporting a fitted tee under a leather jacket, as well as skinny jeans. He had his signature short blonde hairstyle—slick, spiked, and scruffy all at once with just enough style to balance his masculine features and facial hair.

"Jessica, you are looking amazing in that dress! And Bradley, you are looking buff. You must be working out even more!"

All three of them laughed.

"Chica, how are you doing?" Jessica exclaimed. "It's been over a week since I've seen you at the studio. How did everything go with Kyle today?"

"It's been a rough week. As you'd expect. Kyle picked up the last of his belongings today. My first reaction was to burst into tears when he left like some heartbroken girl. But now, I am starting to feel better. I know I ultimately made the right decision."

"Hell yeah, girl! Honestly, screw relationships. They're overrated. You are one of the most resilient and bad-ass people I know," Bradley asserted.

"This seems like the perfect opportunity for a shot!" Jessica chimed in. "What do you guys say?"

"Fine!"

Madison reached for the bottle of Casamigos on the bar cart as well as three silver shot glasses. Jessica immediately raised her shot glass.

"Cheers to a night of uninhibited fun and pleasure. I am ready to relive our wild club days. Let's make this a night to remember!" Jessica declared.

The tequila always hit Madison quickly. She could feel the remaining tension in her body loosen. She reached for the remote to the sound system and turned up the volume, feeling even more emboldened.

The three of them danced and laughed, traversing between the indoor and outdoor entertaining space, welcoming the cool but comfortable April night. They gleefully gossiped for a couple of hours while downing a few more glasses of champagne, discussing everything from the latest in world news to celebrity gossip. Bradley started recounting his latest sexual encounter.

"Well, he was really well-built. Super-fit Hispanic guy with a six-pack, chiseled arms, and thick thighs. Oh, and his ass . . ."

Madison giggled, but before Bradley could get into the juicy details, she stood up, stating assertively, "Okay guys. It's almost eleven. I think it's time to head out."

They chugged their remaining drinks and headed downstairs for the Uber. After a five-minute ride, they arrived at the nightclub and saw that a line had formed around the block.

"Wait, I think I see Denton working the front! Let me see if I can get us in now."

Jessica always seemed to know someone working the front of an event. The trio walked toward the front entrance as Jessica waved her friend down. Denton, tall and thickly built, approached the group. Jessica tossed her hair and leaned forward.

"Hola guapo, it's good to see you! I haven't seen you at the dance studio in a while. How have you been?"

Denton, seemingly a little embarrassed that his secret passion for dance had been exposed, avoided acknowledgment of the comment and directly replied.

"How many?"

Jessica seemed perplexed at the cold response. Madison chimed in, giving a slight smile.

"There's three of us."

"Pull up your tickets and I'll let you guys in now."

They all opened their phones and showed their codes. Denton released the red velvet rope.

"Have fun you guys and be safe."

Madison could hear the throbbing of the music as they entered. The entry hallway was dimly lit by fluorescent tube lights leading to a set of stairs. At the bottom, they pulled back a curtain to expose a huge dance floor already packed with partygoers, briefly illuminated at times by flashing strobe lights overhead. In the middle was a raised DJ booth with a large disco light hanging overhead. On either side of the dance floor, a bar was set against a tall brick wall, dimly lit by similar tube lights. The minimalistic décor had a true basement, underground rave vibe.

The tribal house music started to pick up in intensity, sharp percussion beats slapping Madison's ear drums. She grabbed her friends' hands and led them toward the bar on the left side. Jostling her way to the front, she caught the eye of a bartender with jet-black hair, piercing blue eyes, and chiseled features. He made his way over.

"What can I get you, beautiful?"

"I'll take three tequila sodas with limes and a bottle of water, please."

After the bartender placed down a bottle of water and turned to make the drinks, Madison looked to her side and saw that Jessica had squeezed up right next to her, grabbing her right hand and slipping something into it. She gave Madison a smile and a nod.

"I gave one to Bradley too."

Madison had a feeling Jessica would bring E. The party drug days were mostly behind her, though tonight she wasn't afraid to let her inhibitions run wild. A rush of adrenaline surged through her as she looked around, found that no one was watching, and placed the pill in her mouth, downing it with some of the water.

"No turning back now!"

Jessica looked on with satisfaction. She slipped a pill in her own mouth and swallowed it. By then, the bartender had circled back and placed the cocktails on the bar top. Jessica handed him her credit card, but he shook his head.

"This one's on me. Have fun tonight, ladies."

The man's striking eyes caused Madison to melt where she stood. Jessica gently pulled on her arm and she came to her senses, handing Bradley his drink. Then the trio pushed their way through the line and made their way to the center of the dance floor.

The strobe lights flashed above them as the music picked up power. Madison could feel the energy of the young professional crowd around them. She could sense they were here to escape the stresses of their daily lives and release pent-up energy. Everyone was desperately craving a boost of dopamine.

She thought she recognized someone on the opposite side of the dance floor. A girl about her age with long strawberry-blonde hair. From behind, it looked like Amy. But it couldn't be. Amy was in Connecticut. Madison started to walk in that direction, struck by the similarity, until the girl turned around and kissed a man at her side. Completely different facial features. Madison smirked, finding it laughable how easily fooled she almost was.

But then she remembered she still hadn't responded to Amy's text.

The lights in the room suddenly dimmed, and the crowd cheered in anticipation.

The DJ booth in the center lit up to show a countdown.

Ten. Nine. Eight. Seven. Six.

"Get ready ladies for the night of our lives!" Bradley shouted as he looked toward Madison and Jessica and the number shrank to zero.

Armin van Buuren appeared in the booth above to thunderous applause. Madison could hear the beat building slowly to his song 'Feel Again.' She related to its theme about wasted love, the overwhelming numbness it causes, and the desire to regain feeling in its aftermath.

A sense of pure bliss and a wave of energy took over her as the beat reached its stunning climax. She started to feel a tingling sensation and knew it was the pill kicking in. Dancing to the beat relentlessly with her friends, she became more in tune with her surroundings and soon caught sight of a man to the left of the DJ booth. They locked eyes multiple times as the intensity of the music overtook them.

He was striking—tall, slender, and clean-cut with dark hair. Though he was the opposite of the type of guy Madison typically went after, she felt a strong attraction toward him. Maybe it was just the E, but it felt like something more.

She danced alongside her friends for several more songs until the mysterious man made his way toward her. They locked eyes again, and without even saying a word, the man put his arm around her waist and leaned in for a kiss. It felt like heaven; his lips softly pressed against hers and his tongue moved gently in her mouth. The moment felt better than sex. She didn't want it to end.

The rest of the night was mostly a euphoric blur of continuous highs, dancing, and touching. They continued the fun until the wee hours of the morning, when Madison, her friends, and the stranger finally all found themselves outside of the nightclub. Bradley was insistent on the girls following him to an after-party. Madison peered at her watch through her dilated pupils.

It was nearly 5 a.m.

Coming down and ready to relax and rest, it was time to go home. After leaning over to give one last kiss to Paxton, the tall, enigmatic man she'd met, and exchanging phone numbers, she climbed into an Uber with Jessica and headed home.

The early-morning clouds parted, and the sun shone on another beautiful San Diego spring day as Madison entered her apartment building. She immediately crawled into her bed where she slept for several hours.

She eventually awoke to the sound of a bird chirping outside her window, though she was unable to see it as the blackout curtains completely shut out the light. Feeling tired and with a slight headache, she reached for the phone by her bedside and noticed several new text notifications. It was already noon.

First was a message from Bradley, from just twenty minutes earlier.

Just made it home from the after party! Time to sleep for the next 24 hours! Text me when you're up!

The next message was from Jessica.

Got home safe! Had so much fun last night! Text me later.

Immediately following were several older messages. She still hadn't texted Amy back.

Madison, head still pounding from last night, was about to respond to Amy when she saw her mom calling her. Exhausted and unsure if she wanted to talk, she reluctantly picked up.

"Hi, Mom. How are you? I was just taking a nap."

"Madison, sweetie, there's something I need to—I am so sorry to have to tell you this. . ."

"What is it?"

"Amy. Amy Carlisle." She paused, holding back tears.

"What about Amy, Mom? What's wrong?"

"She's dead."

2

Madison had never felt so alone. How could Amy have been murdered?

Mom told her the story was already top news in Connecticut. Homicides were rare in a wealthy town like Westport. Police had found her around midnight on Friday. Amy had been violently stabbed multiple times and her body found on the side of her hot tub.

The investigation was in the early stages. Robbery? Passion killing? An immediate suspect was not yet identified. The killer left no clues, any footprints left behind were already covered with snow that had steadily fallen throughout the night.

Madison would fly to Connecticut later in the week for the funeral.

She was unsure how to occupy herself in the meantime. She felt a deep emptiness inside, a complete 180 from the euphoric high hours before. It would have been comforting to have someone there to console her. *Kyle.* Part of her was tempted to call him to mend their relationship. But that would be selfish.

Madison knew her mom was concerned about her being alone until she flew home, so it was no surprise when Zane reached out to check on her. He could be a doting brother sometimes. He lived in Los Angeles and arrived home on Monday morning on a red-eye from a business trip. That was when she received a text from him.

Hey— just got into LA. Mom told me what happened with Amy and she's worried about you. Driving to San Diego now.

Mom had asked Zane to drive down. They were close growing up— Zane often felt withdrawn, and Madison was there to help him feel included. As they got older, they kept in touch, but it wasn't the same as when they were younger. Though they lived only two hours apart, it seemed lately they were only connecting during times of tragedy. She last saw her brother three months earlier when their dad passed away.

Madison replied.

Appreciate it. I need to get out of my apartment for some fresh air. Let's meet at Balboa Park. Near the botanical garden. Text me when you're 20 minutes away and I'll head over.

She reluctantly got out of bed to get ready. The warm shower soothed her achy body. She felt exhausted from little sleep over the last two nights and from only eating a bowl of Kraft macaroni and cheese. She couldn't shake the feeling that her life was spinning out of control.

She tried her best to look presentable but gave up after applying minimal make-up. Sweatpants felt like the most comfortable option. A simple t-shirt sounded fine. A messy hair bun would do the trick.

Penelope gently pawed at her feet. Typically, she would either take Penelope to the dog park to play or on a long walk along the bay. Unfortunately, today it would be just a quick walk outside. After feeding her, she reached for an apple on the counter and took a bite. A new text message appeared on her phone.

I'm about 20 minutes away. See you in a few.

She grabbed her keys and headed to the building's garage. She had regrets about agreeing to meet in a public place—the last thing she wanted was to be around other people. At least she would be with someone she trusted, her brother. And getting out in the sun would help.

After arriving at the park, she walked toward the botanical building which housed the gardens. She waited outside for several minutes until she saw her brother approach. He was dressed casually as well, in a white t-shirt, blue jeans, and baseball cap. Zane was tall and handsome. He favored their father with his brown hair and eyes.

Madison walked closer to him and waved.

"Hey, Madison. Barely recognized you. You're usually all dressed up. I don't think I've ever seen you in sweatpants outside of the house."

He reached one of his arms around her. She embraced him with both arms and looked back up at her brother.

"Yeah, can't say I'm feeling all that great. It's been a rough weekend."

"I'm so sorry about Amy. I know how close you guys were. Do they know who murdered her?"

"They don't. Mom said it is a big news story in Connecticut and the investigation is on-going. Possibly a robbery gone wrong. Amy's neighborhood was very wealthy. I just can't believe something like this would happen to her."

"Yeah, it's shocking."

"There are a lot of people that are going to be absolutely devastated. I know her mom is going to be heartbroken. I just can't believe I'm going back home for another funeral. First Dad, now Amy…"

"I know. I worry about Mom being all alone in that house now too.

When you go back, make sure you stay with her. She will appreciate the company even if it isn't under the best circumstances. When do you fly?"

"My flight is on Thursday. Amy's service is on Friday."

"Is Kyle flying back with you?"

"Kyle and I ended things."

"Well, if it makes you feel any better, Kyle wasn't my favorite. Something a little off with him that I couldn't quite put my finger on. I think Dad felt the same way too."

"Why do you say that?"

"Dad never told you? Kyle asked for Dad's permission to marry you late last year. Dad said no."

"Dad never mentioned anything. How did you find out?"

"Mom told me."

Why had Dad not given Kyle his consent?

Zane continued, "Ask Mom when you are home. Sounds like it may have been a blessing in disguise though. I'm always here if you need anything. I know we haven't been the best at keeping in touch but just know I care about you. Hopefully you can distract yourself with other activities to keep your mind off things for a bit. That always helps me when things take a turn."

"Yeah. I've been getting back into dance. Work has been stressful, but what job isn't, right? I think my company likes me, and the pay is good so I'm thankful for that."

"I know Dad was always proud of you for all you accomplished career-wise. I remember when you landed a great-paying job a year before you graduated college, all during a recession when everyone else was struggling to find work. You've always come out on top. I've always looked up to you for that even though I'm two years older."

Madison remembered being one of Zane's biggest advocates growing up, even when he and their parents, especially their dad, didn't always see eye-to-eye. Mom was the more forgiving one. Dad prided himself on being an achiever and tried his best to instill the same ethics in his children. Initially, as hard as Zane would try in school, he didn't excel as quickly as the other kids. As he got older, this led to frustration, which ultimately demotivated him further. When he started missing homework assignments and skipping class, his father became agitated. Dad saw lack of effort as a failure.

The behavior progressively got worse, with Zane developing a more aggressive nature that would often lead to fights at school. This unfortunately spilled into home life with more arguments and fighting—him punching his dad in senior year in high school was the final straw.

Madison had tried to uplift him in every way possible, but there was only so much she could do.

"I've looked up to you as well. I know you struggled in school sometimes, but it was inspiring to see you do something to further yourself when you joined the Army. Even when you worked at Dad's hedge fund for a brief time—" Madison caught herself. She almost forgot he was fired for stealing money from the company. "—And now you have that steady sales job. Not all of us follow the same exact path. And Mom and Dad really grew to admire that too. I know Dad would be happy to see us together right now."

Zane nodded his head in agreement. "I still can't believe he's gone."

She was still wearing the necklace. She grabbed a hold of the key and could feel her dad's presence. He would have loved to join his kids for lunch in the park.

"Well, I don't know about you, but I'm starving. All I've eaten in the past few days is some mac and cheese. I've been an emotional wreck."

"Know a good place we can eat around here?"

"Yes—there's a great Spanish restaurant in the park you have to try. They have some amazing Sangria too that Dad loved. I think this occasion calls for a pitcher."

Madison walked alongside her brother toward the restaurant. She hoped talking about Dad would bring her and Zane closer than ever before.

3

On late Thursday afternoon, Madison ran through the windy streets of New York City toward Grand Central Station.

She clutched her peacoat tightly in one hand and dragged her suitcase in the other as she hurried along the busy sidewalk. It was close to 5 p.m., so people were just getting off work, and the wind was picking up as the sun started to set.

The blustery weather reminded her why she'd moved away from the northeast years ago; she certainly did not miss the raw, unforgiving winters which sometimes spilled into spring. Though the hustle and bustle of the city was typically an exciting change of pace from the relaxed beach vibe of San Diego, right now she wanted nothing more than to arrive at her destination.

Traveling back home to Westport was always such a tedious journey. The six-hour flight cross country was just the start of the trek; she then had to take the AirTrain at JFK Airport, followed by another subway ride, a walk to Grand Central Station, and finally a train to

Westport. It was not an easy day of travel, and the circumstances only made it worse.

She walked the main concourse, marveling at the iconic beauty and grandeur of the building. Shoving her way past throngs of businessmen and tourists, she located the departure board and found her train to Westport—track twelve, departure 5:30 p.m. With fifteen minutes to spare, she grabbed a quick cup of tea from a newsstand and headed toward the track. The swelling crowd was dizzying, throwing her off balance several times.

As Madison walked briskly, she had a strange feeling that someone was following her. She nervously glanced over her shoulder, but nobody stood out. She continued, but once again felt the sensation. Thankfully, her train was in sight. She rapidly increased her pace until she reached the doors of the train, glancing back a final time as she boarded. Again, nothing.

Brushing off the paranoia, she walked down the train car until she found an empty row of seats. After carefully placing her luggage in the storage above, she sat down, already exhausted from the long day of travel. She pulled out her phone and sent a text to her mom.

On the train now in New York City. Should be arriving to Westport at 7 p.m. I'll call you when I'm there. Love you!

She had last seen her mom in January. She wished again that she had been home over the holidays.

Placing her phone and purse on the tray table in front of her, she leaned back in the chair and closed her eyes. Even the train conductor, who loudly announced their departure in five minutes, didn't startle her. She drifted off to sleep immediately. She tried to forget the horrible circumstances that awaited her in Westport, wishing instead she was traveling home to spend time with Amy.

While asleep, a memory of their last summer together before college resurfaced. Amy and Madison both loved the Fourth of July, and they had agreed to celebrate it with a week at Madison's parents' vacation home on Cape Cod. The vacation was a quintessential summer Cape experience filled with long days at the beach, barbeques, shopping in the quaint seaside villages, eating at the best seafood shacks, and dive bar hopping at night. In her dream, both were at the beach on a stunning summer day. Amy was reading a book and Madison was soaking up the afternoon sunshine, with the gentle bay breeze whipping at their hair. At one point, Amy turned to face her and gave a gentle and sincere smile. Their friend Dawn was also there. Zane too.

The picture-perfect setting slowly faded, and she gradually opened her eyes, desperately wishing she hadn't awoken from her dream. She felt as though Amy was with her and didn't want to leave that moment of serenity. Everything felt so peaceful and wonderful. This joy was overcome by disorientation as she came back to consciousness. She realized Amy was dead.

The train lights were off. Though it was dark outside, she could vaguely see the train was zipping through a suburban area; they were well outside the city by now. Madison peeked to her left and saw that no one had taken the seat beside her even though the train car was roughly three-quarters full.

Feeling relieved that she was one of the lucky ones, she was about to close her eyes again when she saw a neatly folded piece of white paper on the tray directly next to her purse. She reached overhead to turn on the light and hesitantly picked up the piece of paper, unfolding it slowly. To her surprise, the note only had two words handwritten in bold, capital letters.

HOT TUB

Hot tub? Did this have something to do with Amy? Her body was found there. She looked around; there was a businessman in his mid-40s in the row across from her, by the window. He was typing away enthusiastically on his laptop, clearly not paying attention. Directly behind her was a mother with her young son; the mom had dozed off and her head pressed against the train window, while the son was playing on an iPad.

Madison debated asking the people around her if they saw someone place the note on her tray but ultimately decided not to. It wasn't like it was a threat or anything. She sat for a few moments in confusion. Was she jumping to conclusions assuming it referred to where Amy's body was found?

It couldn't be related—it had to be a scrap of paper that had fallen as someone walked by.

The conductor made another announcement on the loudspeaker.

"Westport. Five minutes until arrival."

She tucked the note inside her peacoat and gathered her belongings. She stood and reached for the luggage above her seat. As she walked toward the train car exit, she anxiously looked around again, that feeling of unease still heavy in her gut. She reached for her phone to call Jane as the train came to a stop.

"Hi, Mom. I'm walking off the train now. Should be in the pick-up area in the next five minutes."

"Okay, honey. See you in a few minutes!"

Madison headed down the stairwell leading to the main train station terminal. Once outside, she saw the lights of her mother's SUV as it pulled up beside her on the curb.

Jane immediately stepped out of the car and gave her daughter a warm embrace, holding her tightly. After she released her, Madison loaded her luggage into the trunk and climbed into the warm car, ready to escape the chill outside.

"Mom, how is it still cold here? This isn't spring! I don't know why you still like it out here. Come move west with me."

"I know. You know I love San Diego, but it's just so far from my life here."

This was a regular conversation between them; Madison knew it was a lost cause. Being away from the house she had grown so accustomed to would be nearly impossible for Mom; the house had been passed down in the family for several generations. It was a historic colonial charmer, recently updated and situated on a lake, a house her parents could have never afforded on their own.

After fifteen minutes of winding through the narrow tree-lined streets of Westport, they drove down the long driveway toward their home. Once the car came to a stop in the garage, Madison grabbed her suitcase from the trunk and entered the house, walked through the mudroom, and into the kitchen. She still wasn't accustomed to the silence that pervaded her once lively childhood home.

"You must be exhausted from a long day of traveling. I know it's getting late but, if you're still hungry, I made you your favorite—chicken marsala."

"Thanks! I am starving, so sounds perfect."

Jane grabbed a plate of already prepared food from the fridge and heated it in the microwave as Madison sat down at the large kitchen island. She glanced around. Not much had changed since she was last home, though in one of the kitchen shelf cut-outs, near the farmhouse kitchen sink, she did notice a handful of newly framed photos that hadn't been there before.

One was of Zane in his Army uniform—he looked proud and confident. It was before he was deployed to Iraq, when things took a turn. On the third deployment he witnessed his close friend killed by a roadside bomb. He eventually was medically discharged from the Army due to PTSD.

Madison saw that several of the other photos were of Dad.

Immediately, Madison felt a sense of love sweep over her, though the pain of her dad's passing three months ago still hurt immensely. She had been working to replace that grief by remembering the good times. He was a gentle soul that led with compassion. He was Madison's biggest cheerleader, encouraging her to follow her passions while also teaching the importance of academics. This was how she was able to juggle creative pursuits like dance with her professional career.

Dad had been sick for a few years with colon cancer, a time that still haunted her, though she tried to remember him when he was healthy and in good spirits. After he had been in remission, she was hopeful that life for him would gradually turn back to normal. Then he had been diagnosed again, this time with stage four cancer, and his health rapidly deteriorated. He passed away three months later. But not from the cancer.

"I love those new photos of Dad you added over there," Madison said, pointing toward the shelf. "Especially the one in front of the Cape Cod house. When was that taken?"

Wiping away a few quick tears, Jane quietly replied, "I know. I miss him every day. That picture was taken around the New Year. Right before the robbery…"

Madison would never forget the day she received a call from Mom saying that Dad was in serious condition at Cape Cod Hospital. At first, she suspected it was the cancer. She was horrified to learn that a robber broke into the Cape Cod house and beat Dad while Mom was grocery shopping. Madison took the first flight she could back east with Kyle before Dad passed away.

Jane paused then continued, "I still can't believe that someone did this all over some jewelry, just so they could sell it for drug money. To think someone could be so cold to kill a husband and a father over that. It breaks my heart."

The robber ended up being a well-known drifter around town who needed money for his next fix. He was found on the streets the next day near the Parker home with the stolen jewelry in his jacket. He was immediately arrested and charged even though he repeatedly denied involvement.

Madison noticed in one of the photos Dad was wearing the gold key pendant necklace.

She recalled being by her father's bedside in the hospital that final day. He had trouble speaking, but he grabbed hold of the necklace he was wearing and handed it to her. He tried to whisper something, but she couldn't quite understand what he was saying. Madison figured he wanted to give his daughter one final gift.

An hour later, Madison and her mom went to the hospital cafeteria to eat. Kyle had gone out to get more flowers for her dad's bedside, and Zane was on a conference call downstairs. Suddenly, she'd received a call from the nurse saying that Dad had gone into cardiac arrest. By the time she and Mom had rushed back upstairs, he had passed.

"Mom, you know how I felt that day. Something just didn't sit right with me. If Dad's vital signs were improving, then how did he suddenly go into cardiac arrest? And that mysterious needle prick on the back of his arm. We never found out what it was from. Maybe one of the nurses had a misstep…"

"I know it was all such a shock. But the toxicology came back negative. It wasn't an accidental poisoning. Your father died from his injuries. His body was already so weak from the cancer."

Madison still had her suspicions that they never got to the bottom of what really happened.

Jane gazed at the photos as the microwave timer sounded. She reached for the food she had prepared for her daughter.

"I hope it's as good as I used to make it, dear. Enjoy!"

She scarfed down the chicken marsala as if she hadn't eaten in months. In truth, she hadn't since the breakfast sandwich at the airport in San Diego. Jane sat beside her daughter as she devoured the food.

"I know we haven't had time to speak about it yet, but Dad left some substantial assets. Roughly half of his estate will be split between you and your brother. Thankfully he had a will established soon after you kids were born. Dad had mentioned he was working on an amendment to the will, but we were never able to locate it. The amount you each will be receiving will be one million dollars. It will of course take some time to settle."

Madison's heart dropped. She knew that amount of money would be immensely helpful. She could use it to pursue her passions, something Dad would have wanted for her. Possibly start a business venture with Jessica and open more dance studios. Use it to buy a house. Still, she wanted nothing more than to have Dad back. No amount of money would change that.

"Dad had such a big heart. I wasn't expecting anything. I'm speechless. I want to use the money for something that would make him proud."

"I know you will. You have always been just as responsible with money as he was. I just wish you were home this time under better circumstances. First Dad, now Amy."

"Is there any update on who killed Amy? Did I tell you she sent me a text that night she was killed? She told me she missed me and asked when I was coming home next. I never thought it would be for her funeral..."

Before Madison could finish her thought, she caught of glimpse of the TV in the living room. It was the local evening news. The headline *Local Westport Murder Shocks Town: Killer Still At Large* flashed on the screen. Madison reached for the remote on the kitchen island and turned up the volume. The correspondent was reporting outside of Amy's home.

"Very early Saturday morning, the body of a woman was found outside her lavish Westport, Connecticut home in the snow, brutally stabbed multiple times. The victim has now been identified as thirty-five-year-old Amy Carlisle. Before her murder, she had phoned police to report an intruder inside her house. Unfortunately, it took authorities twenty minutes to arrive at the scene due to the snowstorm. By the time they arrived, Amy was found unresponsive.

The motive for the vicious murder is still unknown, as is the identity of the killer, who is still at large. A funeral service will be held for the victim tomorrow at Saint Patrick's Church in Westport. Anyone with any information is urged to contact Westport Police immediately..."

Madison shut off the television. She couldn't bear to hear more.

"After the service at the church tomorrow, there will be a small remembrance celebration." Jane paused. "At Elizabeth's house."

Madison looked at her mom and felt nervous. She didn't want to confront the reality that Amy was gone.

4

Madison and Jane entered the cobblestone church as the bells rang overhead. It was 10 a.m.

They were soon welcomed by the priest, who was greeting mourners at the door. It was a remarkably mild day, close to seventy degrees, and a far contrast from the cold start to the spring season. The sun was beginning to shine through the gray clouds, which flooded the colorful stained-glass windows with light.

As they walked down the center aisle, Madison immediately noticed the majestic gold-encrusted archways, rows of oak pews, marble floors, and stunning murals. A large statue depicting the crucifixion of Jesus hung from the wall above the pulpit.

Then she looked below the statue and saw it. The open casket. Amy was dressed in a flowing white gown, her long, strawberry-blonde hair styled beautifully. From this distance, Amy appeared like her normal self. It was difficult for Madison to fathom that her close friend was no longer alive. Countless people had already filled the pews, but Jane was able to locate an opening in the center. They carefully nudged their way in.

Madison closed her eyes and took a deep breath. Then she looked around and spotted a few familiar faces, including her friend Dawn Presley. Seated at the front of the church was Amy's mother, Elizabeth, gently sobbing next to her other relatives. She also noticed Amy's stepfather, Alexander, seated a couple of rows behind Elizabeth. The two had been divorced for close to ten years, very soon after Amy graduated from college. Amy never had the opportunity to meet her birth father; he abandoned her soon after she was born.

Madison couldn't keep her eyes off Elizabeth—even in her own pain, she couldn't imagine the pain that woman was feeling over losing her only child. She looked heartbroken, likely still in shock that her daughter was viciously killed. Madison wanted nothing more than to wrap her arms around her in a tight embrace. After the services, she had to speak with Elizabeth to offer her support. They'd grown close over the years and she considered her a second mom of her own.

The mass finally began, a somber affair, though beautifully orchestrated. Most notable was the sound of the church choir that echoed throughout the church halls, singing a haunting and emotional hymn that was uplifted by the sweet, gentle melody of a flute. Madison recalled Amy played the flute growing up. She took this as a sign from her friend.

Though she wasn't a devout Catholic herself, she found the entire mass to be profoundly moving, filled as it was with music and prayer. Following holy communion service, she saw Elizabeth make her way to the pulpit. Amy's mom delivered a gut-wrenching speech that left the church in tears.

"I am heartbroken at the tremendous loss of my dear daughter,

Amy, who has been taken from us much too soon. Her unconditional love, optimistic outlook on life, kindness, and generosity permeated every aspect of her being. She displayed enthusiasm in every facet of her life, whether in her love for music or dedication to her career. Guided by her faith and spirituality, she had a thirst for exploration and adventure at an early age that followed her into her adult life."

Amy's mom continued, recounting numerous stories of her daughter's important life milestones and influential people she met along the way. "There are many of Amy's friends here today that she treasured deeply." Elizabeth paused and made eye contact with Madison.

A few tears streamed down Madison's cheek as she too recalled some of her dearest memories with Amy, especially their favorite vacation spot on the Cape. She briefly lost herself in the moment, still in disbelief that her good friend was lying motionless in front of the altar before her.

After the service and burial, she and her mom drove to Elizabeth's house, just five minutes from the church.

Around ten cars were already parked in the driveway and on the street. Upon entering, she saw that the family had placed countless framed photos of Amy on tables along the main foyer, reflecting her vibrant life from childhood to adulthood. A guest book lay nearby, which she signed.

Eventually, Madison saw Elizabeth in the kitchen, putting out some sandwiches and light refreshments. Madison immediately walked over, gave her a hug, and held her tight, not wanting to let go.

"I'm so sorry, Elizabeth. That speech you gave moved me to tears. Amy would have been proud."

"Amy loved you so much. You were always her most special friend."

"She meant the world to me too. She was always there for me. She helped me so much when my dad passed. Taught me how to laugh again."

"I know, she wanted to make sure you were okay. She was always one to bring light to even the darkest situations."

After chatting for several minutes, Elizabeth was pulled aside by another grieving family member. Madison, now standing alone, saw Alexander Carlisle approaching. Amy's stepfather had also been Dad's business partner. They'd gotten to know each other well when their daughters became close friends in grade school. After working several high-profile jobs at various investment banks in New York City, they started a private hedge fund together. They ran it for multiple years until Madison's dad had to drastically cut down his hours due to the stage four cancer diagnosis.

"Hi, Madison. It's been awhile. I wanted to express my condolences."

She hadn't seen Alexander in the years after Dad started working part-time. He hadn't even come to Dad's funeral, though he did send the family flowers. He had been largely absent from Amy's life after his divorce from Elizabeth.

"Thanks. I am sorry for your loss as well."

"I regret not staying closer with Amy after the divorce. I still loved her. I also wanted to express my condolences for your father. I never got a chance to tell you in person how sorry I was for his unexpected passing."

Though talking about her dad usually brought her joy, she felt a little uneasy. She was feeling overwhelmed by Amy's passing and the prospect of discussing her dad with someone she hadn't spoken to in years. Madison felt bad about wanting to keep the conversation short because Alexander seemed sympathetic and kind, but luckily she saw her friend Dawn wave at her from the living room.

"Again, thanks so much Alexander. I appreciate your kind words. We would have loved to see you at my dad's funeral but appreciated the flowers you sent. I hope our families can come together and offer each other support. Please keep in touch."

She politely walked away, having little energy to engage in small talk with someone she barely knew anymore. She joined in a conversation Dawn was having with some other acquaintances from high school.

"Glad we saved you from Alexander. I've never been a huge fan of him," Dawn proclaimed as Madison entered the circle.

Dawn was a tall, curvy woman with a modelesque face and a larger-than-life personality. Now a budding women's fashion designer in the city, she mentioned how excited she was to be showcasing her latest collection in Manhattan next month. Dawn was a good friend of Madison's in high school, though Dawn was always competitive with her for Amy's attention. Dawn's parents owned a lavish vacation property across the water from Madison's house in Cape Cod, so the three girls would often spend time there.

In college, Dawn and Madison would mainly connect when they were home for the summer. After Madison moved to San Diego, however, their friendship faded, mostly due to the distance and their hectic work schedules. Dawn had traveled out to California once when Madison first moved there, saying at the time it was solely to visit her, but Madison knew it coincided with a business trip to Los Angeles. But even though the two had gradually lost touch over the years, Madison was excited to see her today.

Much like other guests at the house, they exchanged hugs, condolences, and utter shock at the murder. Both expressed their bewilderment as to who could have done this to Amy; there were no people in her immediate circle that they were aware of who harbored any sort of resentment or hatred toward her. Dawn mentioned how she had seen Amy a few weeks before, but nothing in her behavior seemed out of the ordinary.

After chatting for several more minutes, Dawn found an opportunity to pull Madison aside so they were alone.

"Amy did mention to me a few weeks ago that she had set up everything in her house, except for unpacking a few boxes in the attic. I know she was still trying to figure out what to do with that space. I heard she was hiding in the attic before she was murdered. What do you think about us going to her house later to see if we can find anything?"

Madison hesitated, not wanting to seem like she was intruding or meddling where she didn't belong. "I don't know. We are here to celebrate Amy's life. I don't think it's our place to snoop around. Plus the police would have already discovered any evidence. It's not like we are going to find anything new . . ."

Dawn grabbed her hand. "I totally hear what you are saying. But Amy would want us to know the truth about what happened. We won't be long. I'm going with or without you."

Dawn wasn't joking. Once she had her mind made up, there was no turning back.

"Fine, I'll go. But we can't break into the house. I'll only do it if there's a window or door open."

"Deal. This is wrapping up soon anyways so let's head out soon."

After mingling for ten more minutes, Madison let Mom know that she was going out with Dawn to grab a drink.

Soon, they were parked on the street outside Amy's house. Yellow crime scene tape surrounded the property. There didn't appear to be any crime scene investigators around. It was a Friday afternoon, so maybe they'd left for the day.

Both looked around and, seeing no one, walked to the front door. Locked. All the front windows were closed.

"Well, Dawn. That takes care of that. Let's get out of here."

"We didn't check out the back yet. Come over here around the side yard."

Dawn has already disappeared around the corner.

She followed and saw the pool in the backyard. And the hot tub—where Amy's body was found. She didn't want to get any closer, feeling there may still be blood stains.

"Madison, the back door is open!"

She couldn't believe it. Dawn had already disappeared inside.

"Wait up!" Madison screamed.

After walking through the living area, Madison could hear footsteps going up the stairwell. She followed her friend up the staircase, eventually going through the master bedroom toward the closet.

She was surprised to learn that there was a tiny door in the closet that led to a third story. Both girls climbed through the doorway and progressed up the narrow stairwell to the attic. Once at the top, the sun streamed through the patio door. Other than a few unopened boxes, the attic felt eerily empty and lifeless.

Madison walked to the patio door and stepped out to get a breath of fresh air. She leaned over and saw the expansive backyard, pool, and hot tub below. Immediately, she envisioned the night of the murder, imagining the terror that Amy must have felt. She remembered the note she received on the train. When she turned around, Dawn had already ripped open one of the boxes.

"So, when I was on the train to Connecticut, someone left a note on my tray table that said *hot tub*. Do you think it has any connection to Amy?"

"Is that all the note said?"

"Yes."

"Probably just a coincidence. I wouldn't worry about it. Doesn't sound threatening."

Dawn was continuing to sort through the boxes.

Madison was getting anxious they were being too intrusive. "Hey, I doubt we will find anything. The police would have already found any relevant evidence. Let's go back downstairs."

Dawn pulled out a red sequin outfit with a matching wig and proclaimed, "Oh my gosh, remember when Amy dressed as Cher in high school?"

Admiring the outfit, they both laughed. Dawn continued to dig through the boxes, while Madison spotted a smaller box in a dark corner of the room. She walked over and reluctantly opened it, slowly digging through its contents.

Madison stumbled upon their high school yearbook from senior year and opened it. After skimming the notes other classmates wrote Amy, she landed on hers, which took up an entire page. Inside jokes that only the two of them would understand. Dawn would often get jealous for not being included.

She found another signature page toward the end and saw Zane's note.

> *Amy,*
> *I hope you have a memorable summer before college this Fall. I've never told you, but I've always had a crush on you. I would love to go on a date sometime.*
> *Zane Parker*

Dawn called over to her. "Find anything?"

"Just Amy's high school yearbook." She pointed to Zane's note.

"Remember this?"

Dawn laughed. "Oh my gosh, we were so mean to your brother that summer after finding out he had a crush on Amy. I feel like we traumatized him with that prank. It was all Amy's idea!"

"I remember you were mad and yelled at Amy and I earlier that day on the beach for feeling excluded. I think she came up with the prank to bring us three girls closer."

On the Fourth of July after high school graduation, Madison and Dawn blindfolded Zane in the basement of her Cape Cod house. They brought him outside where Amy was waiting. Amy pretended she had a crush on him and had him take off all his clothes including his underwear. She then asked for a kiss and as Zane leaned forward, they pushed a dead fish to his lips. He ripped off the blindfold immediately and stood there naked, wide-eyed after slowly coming to the realization it was a joke.

Madison couldn't shake the memory of his petrified expression as they all stood around him laughing. As one of Zane's biggest supporters, he probably felt Madison betrayed him in that moment. "I should have stopped her when she started caressing his naked body. Not something I wanted to see someone doing to my brother. I deserved him slapping me."

Dad ended up punishing him for the slap, something she felt guilty about. She got a pit in her stomach every time she thought of her failure to protect her brother that day.

Madison gently bowed her head. Thankfully, her and Zane had recovered from that incident years ago and hadn't spoken about it since. She closed the yearbook and placed it back in the box. A memory worth forgetting.

"Let's go, Dawn. I told you we wouldn't find anything."

5

The basement was cold and musty.

It was lunchtime and stacks of childhood boxes waited for her, a task Mom decided needed her attention, seeing as she had decided to stay in Connecticut for a few weeks. Her boss, Kristin Tate, approved the remote work. It was daunting, deciding what to keep, what to throw away.

There were photos from birthdays, graduations, and proms, one taken outside her house before high school graduation. A happy memory. She graduated in the top five percent of her class. Dad was so proud. Another photo was a group shot in front of a limo, junior prom. Her drunken prom date aggressively forced himself on her at the beach after-party. She had pushed him off successfully, but he'd driven away in a rage. He was arrested that night for a DUI. He blamed her, of course. Dad was furious and fought with his father. Not a great moment.

The good and the bad experiences helped shape who she was, yes, but some could stay in the box.

Her yearbook lay beneath the photos. It was bound in fake leather. Hardcover with color photos. Madison flipped to her senior photo, a likable picture. She'd blossomed that spring and started attracting the attention of others. She'd chosen a quote from Martin Luther King, Jr.—*Our lives begin to end the day we become silent about things that matter.*

The words still resonated with her. Beneath, she listed some of her favorite activities: dance, tennis, and writing. Writing. How could she forget about her love for writing? Seemed a distant memory now.

In the corner of the basement sat a large shoe box with big black letters written in Sharpie—*KEEP OUT*. She used to hide that box under her bed. Back then, it was for her eyes only. She knew exactly what it contained. Hopefully, Mom hadn't gone through it.

Opening the box slowly, she was happy to see that nothing appeared missing. It was filled with countless notes, poems, journal entries, and short stories. She dreamed of publishing one of those stories one day. The title, *Whispers*, was in bold, italic letters using a cheesy font she convinced herself was cool back in eighth grade.

She started reading through the first few pages about a woman named Claire who is tormented by a supernatural force in her lakeside home in New Hampshire. One day, she finds a mysterious key in the house. During a seance with her friend, a stack of newspapers falls from the table and an article about a young woman named Madeline missing for two months appears. Madeline looks like Claire and is a graduate student where her husband Warren teaches. She is wearing a necklace in the newspaper photo. Claire tracks down the missing woman's mother. While in Madeline's bedroom, Claire notices a different picture of Madeline wearing the same necklace. Her mother describes how Madeline's dad gifted it to her and told her it had magical powers.

Whispers guide Claire to find a locked box hidden in her husband's desk drawer at home. Using the key, she finds the missing woman's necklace inside. She remembers a few months ago she had suspected her husband had been cheating on her since he had been arriving home late. Claire confronts Warren and he admits to an affair with the missing woman but is unaware of what happened. He suddenly smashes Claire's head with the box and tries to drown her in their lake outside. The missing woman's body surfaces and Warren goes into shock before eventually drowning. Claire survives and places the necklace around Madeline's body, which brings her back to life.

Madison read through a few more pages before setting the story down. What happened to her imagination? The creative energy that radiated through her when she was younger had faded. This story she wrote was a reminder of the talent she once had, one she hoped was not dead. She refused to believe that side of her was lost forever.

Her phone rang. It was Kristin Tate.

"Hey, Madison. Hope it's going okay in Connecticut. Again, I am so sorry about the loss of your friend, Amy. I saw you were online earlier and if you have a second, I have a favor to ask. Regarding the presentation you sent out this morning, Jared redlined basically every other word. I tried to talk it through with him, but he's demanding his feedback be incorporated by close of business today. Do you think you could look at it?"

Jared Demange was the director of her department. He seemed to enjoy critiquing everything she did, never offering support. Nothing was ever good enough.

"Of course. I'll look right now and let you know if I have any questions. I'll get a revision out today."

"Thanks. Please let me know if I can help in any way."

She looked down at the box once more containing her various writings. She longed for a creative outlet, something to escape the monotony of corporate life. Instead, she had to put her energy toward revising a presentation unnecessarily. It felt meaningless and uninspiring.

Before closing the box, she grabbed the copy of *Whispers* and proceeded up the staircase to the main level of the house. She intended to pack the story in her suitcase and bring it back with her to San Diego. It still could be published.

After opening her laptop again, Madison was disgruntled at some of the comments Jared left on the presentation.

> *Why would you include this?*
> *Bad choice of words. Reword completely.*
> *Didn't I give you this same feedback last time?*

She was not surprised. He was often vague with his criticism and left little room for constructive feedback.

Bradley messaged her on Slack after noticing she was online.

Just wanted to check in on you. Hope you're doing okay. Again, I'm so sorry about Amy.

Madison responded.

Thanks. Service was a few days ago. Can't believe she's gone. Kristin has been totally understanding. But Jared is up to his usual ways.

Bradley was typing a response.

Well, don't let him get to you. Jared will never change. Focus on you. Allow yourself time to grieve.

Madison just wanted to get the presentation update out of the way.

That afternoon, she edited it and worked until 6 p.m. before submitting the revision. Frustrated, she closed her laptop. After putting on her workout clothes and AirPods, she called for her mom who was in the kitchen.

"I'm going to go out for a run. I should be back in an hour. Do you want me to pick anything up for dinner on my way?"

"Sounds good, honey. I have dinner covered tonight. Making baked chicken, rice, and veggies. Should be ready by the time you are home."

She stepped out the front door to begin her jog. Exercise always seemed to help clear her mind. Today's song choice, Seal's 'Crazy', provided much-needed nostalgia. She sang along to the melodic and soulful vocals, trying to mimic his characteristic rasp, as she ran.

After about half an hour, she reached the outside of Westport High School. It had been a while since she had been back, but not much seemed to have changed since she graduated. The parking lot was mostly empty as students and teachers had left for the day. She ran past the outside of the school auditorium and slowed her pace before stopping.

A memory from freshman year resurfaced. She had rehearsed for weeks for the school musical *Grease* after Amy encouraged her to audition. Amy helped her rehearse her lines and prepare as much as possible for the lead role of Sandy. At the end of the school day when rehearsals were just beginning, she stood outside waiting to be called.

Initially, she pictured Amy cheering her on. But with each minute that passed she grew more anxious. She was confident with the dance numbers but apprehensive with her singing ability.

What happened if she stumbled through her lines or even worse was off-key for one of the songs? She imagined taking center stage in front of her other classmates with a frozen look on her face. Suddenly, she started to doubt herself and without explanation, stepped out of line and walked home. She never auditioned.

What seemed like a small decision at the time had a domino effect. She quit the band after sophomore year. Junior year she gave up on dance competitions. And halfway through senior year, she stepped down as editor-in-chief of her high school newspaper. All so she could focus on her academics. Though she had participated in honor societies and continued to excel in school, leaving those creative endeavors behind created a void in her life. It was as if she was letting go of a part of her identity.

Despite this, she still entered college with the ambition that she would major in journalism. But even that veered off course after the first semester when she elected to pursue business instead with a minor in biology. Everyone in her circle, from family to school counselors, told her business was the safe route and that she would be more likely to secure a stable job. And make more money. Ironically, it was the minor that likely helped her secure the biotech job.

These decisions paved the way for where she was today. Granted she had a secure job with a good salary, but at what cost? She was left wondering if it was worth giving up her passions.

As Madison walked the perimeter of the auditorium, she imagined where she would be today had she decided to go through with the audition for the school musical freshman year. Maybe she would have shined and moved to Hollywood to become an actress or professional dancer. It was a possibility that she wouldn't have given up her other artistic interests.

She thought about how things may have been different if she hadn't doubted herself and instead listened to Amy's encouraging words. She remembered the dance numbers in the musical she rehearsed for weeks, thankful she had a friend like Jessica who encouraged her to return to dance as an adult. She reached for her phone in her pocket and called Jessica. She answered.

"Hey. Just spoke to Bradley. Heard Amy's funeral was a few days ago. I'm so sorry."

"Thanks. Could use one of your dance classes right about now."

"I'll get those hips swaying in no time."

"How are things at The Heat?"

"Studio has been busier than ever. We miss you."

"Miss you too. I'm outside my high school right now. Just had a memory of this musical I was supposed to audition for freshman year, *Grease*. I chickened out. I think it was the catalyst for me giving up on dance competitions junior year."

"If I knew you back then I would have pushed you on stage and forced you to do it. You're an amazing dancer."

Madison smiled. "Funny you say that. Amy was that same force of encouragement for me growing up. Thank you for reintroducing me to dance."

"Chica, anything for you. It's never too late to pick something up again you once loved. I see such a bright future for you."

They chatted for a few more minutes before saying goodbye.

Madison looked once more at the school as tears streamed down her face. She wished Amy was still alive. Turning, she ran back home.

Her path and circumstances turned out different than she expected. Amy should still be alive and there was nothing Madison could do to bring her back. But there was a glimmer of hope that she still had time to change course of her own life.

6

Dad's old office at home. Exactly how she remembered it. Posters of his favorite bands growing up—Led Zeppelin and Pink Floyd. Science fiction and fantasy books lined the two bookshelves around his desk. Baseball cards were neatly organized in binders. Dad had made a binder for Madison growing up. She pretended to show interest.

Everything in there had a memory. A story.

Madison sat down at his desk. The room still smelled like him. A robin landed on the windowsill outside and started chirping. She opened the desk drawer and saw several folders, one large one labeled *Elite Investments*, the name of Dad's hedge fund. There were several pages of paper inside. She opened it.

It looked like work emails and financial statements. Toward the back of the folder, she saw several pages were paperclipped together with a yellow sticky note on top labeled *Zane*. She became curious.

The first page was a printed email from Amy's stepfather, Alexander

Carlisle, to his company partner William Parker. The email read:

> William-
>
> As we recently discussed in person, I am becoming increasingly concerned with your son fraudulently using investor money. Zane has been misusing investor funds for personal gain and wealth since joining the firm as a bookkeeper.
>
> I have been compiling the evidence and records that prove without a doubt how he has taken thousands of dollars of our clients' funds.
>
> This is an egregious breach of our business code of conduct and it cannot be tolerated.
>
> Though he is your son and I know you had the best intentions for employing him after he was medically discharged from the military, if you choose to do nothing about this, I will have to let him go myself.
>
> In my good conscience, I can't let one of our investors be hurt by his malicious and selfish acts. After this has been settled, you and I will need to discuss further how we reimburse those clients he stole from.
>
> I hope that you will soon do the right thing.
> Sincerely,
> Alexander Carlisle

Madison looked at the date of the email and noted it was around the same time Zane had been fired from the hedge fund. The next page was a reply from her father.

> *Alexander-*
> *I'm sorry that this went on for as long as it did. I could have never imagined Zane would do something like this. I only wanted to help him.*
> *As much as I love my son, I know the right thing to do is terminate his employment.*
> *I will take care of this personally.*
> *William Parker*

The next several pages were bank statements from Elite Investments. She noticed a few of the transactions were circled with red marker. It looked like funds were being moved from the company account to Zane's personal account. Some were worth several thousand dollars. There were also emails from various clients to Zane requesting money withdrawals from their investment accounts. Angry client emails followed complaining about a lack of response. Emails from a few of the company's vendors complaining about unpaid bills. There were also several other bank transaction sheets showing lavish restaurant and travel purchases.

Madison was in shock. She knew Zane was fired for stealing money from the company, but Dad and Mom never told her he was fired for embezzling *thousands* of dollars of investor's money. Maybe her parents had kept it secret for fear it would further divide the family and alienate Zane even more. She also wondered if the stress caused by her brother contributed to their father's cancer reemerging.

They were so close growing up. She'd always stood up and tried to see the good in him. Why didn't he ever tell her about this? He used to confide in her about everything, even when he did something wrong.

Madison grabbed the folder and ran out of the office. Mom was in the family room watching TV.

"Mom, turn off the TV."

"What's wrong?"

"This is what's wrong."

She handed the stack of papers to Mom. Jane glanced at them and realized what they contained.

"Madison—we were trying to protect your relationship with your brother. We didn't want this to ruin it."

"I get that. But I have the right to know the truth. Especially if Zane tried to cheat Dad like that. I thought when you guys said he was fired for stealing money, maybe he stole some money out of the company cash box. Not some elaborate embezzlement scheme."

"I get why you are upset, sweetie. Even though we were mad, Zane was already so alienated. You were one of the few people close to him. We didn't want him to lose you too…"

"I really wish you told me." She paused. "Speaking of things I wish you told me, Zane mentioned Kyle asked Dad for my hand in marriage. Is that true?"

"It is."

"And what did Dad say?"

"He told Kyle you two should work on things before taking that next step. Dad knew you were unsure if you wanted to stay with Kyle. You two seemed to be growing apart."

"So, he said no?"

"In a gentler way of course. We've always wanted what's best for you."

Madison appreciated that her parents recognized how she felt about Kyle. She also now understood why they didn't go into details about her brother being fired from Dad's company. But now she felt a deeper sense of betrayal. She was unsure if she would ever be able to trust Zane again.

7

Madison pulled into the work parking lot ten minutes late for the meeting, still tired from the long flight back to San Diego yesterday.

She grabbed her belongings, ran through the entrance, and darted up the stairs to the second floor. After grabbing a quick cup of coffee and nearly spilling it all over herself, she headed down the executive hallway toward the meeting room. On the other side of the glass doors, Jared stood in front of the room lecturing what he often referred to as his "subordinates," likely about some mandate needed in the next few hours. Though he was tall and strikingly handsome with short curly blonde hair, the sight of him made Madison feel nauseous. She regained her strength once she saw Kristin and Bradley seated at the conference table.

She tried to enter the room gracefully, but the door was at the front of the room and all the seats at the table were occupied. Several chairs sat vacant on the periphery. She quietly sat in one close to the door. Jared paused.

"So nice of you to join us, Madison," he scolded. "You're late."

She looked up and gave a fake smile, knowing how unnecessary it was for him to call her out in a room full of people, especially given the difficult few months she had been through. She knew he was fully aware.

"Traffic," she replied.

After staring in her direction awkwardly, Jared continued. She mostly tuned him out, the best coping strategy. He was brought in from a competitor with extensive biotech experience scaling research drugs into commercialized medicine. Sounded nice on paper, but he was rude, demanding, combative, and often dismissive of alternative ideas. She tried to win him over through hard work but after numerous, blatant disrespects, it was obvious he would never change. He had not been shy about letting others know how unhappy he was in his marriage. Unfortunately, his misplaced anger was beginning to impact the company culture she once loved and admired.

Her phone lit up with a text message from Kristin.

Hey, I'll remind Jared later that you arrived back in town late last night and that is why you were late to the meeting. He should not have called you out like that. I'm so sorry!

Another text from Bradley.

What an ass! Jared is honestly the worst! I don't understand how he is still at this company. Glad you barely acknowledged him. That passive-aggressive smile was EVERYTHING.

Madison let out a big smile, and she looked over to see Bradley smiling back. His confidence and coolness were infectious. She would not have been able to make it through the past year without him cheering her on.

Jared finally wrapped up the meeting, but not before turning to her once more. "Oh, and Madison, we have an executive meeting at 4 p.m. today and I need you to present the update on your account. The executives want to hear the latest from you now that we have FDA approval. Please have this month's financials updated as well. Send the slides to me one hour before the meeting today by 3 p.m."

"I can provide a status update but may not have the financials updated at such short notice. It usually takes several days to compile all the information. Would that be okay?"

He had a habit of setting ridiculous and exhausting deadlines. She understood that sometimes last-minute requests would arise from senior leadership, however, the frequency of his requests were out of control, and often unnecessary.

"I need the financials updated as well. Please get it done."

She could immediately feel her heart sink and her blood pressure spike. The executive meeting was likely planned weeks in advance. She could have easily prepared the material before leaving town for Amy's funeral. Now she had to squeeze several days' worth of work into a few hours.

Anxiety rushed through her body. Preparedness was something she prided herself on, but it was no use pushing back. Her concerns would be largely ignored, and likely only make the situation worse.

Everyone in the room engaged in small talk as the meeting ended. She took a deep breath and settled herself. Anxiety gave way to confidence. She was, after all, talented and good under pressure, two attributes that rubbed on Jared's nerves. She would give a successful presentation this afternoon, even with the short notice.

She postponed her morning and afternoon meetings and buckled into her desk. 4 p.m., bring it on. At 11 a.m., Bradley checked on her, a vase of white lilies in hand.

"I'm so sorry about Amy. I can't imagine what you're going through. Jared really is a dick for calling you out like that especially when he knows you've had a difficult few months. Is there anything I can do to help you prepare? I'm good with the finance part and can help pull the numbers for you."

"You're so sweet. And these lilies are breathtaking. You're busy enough. I should be able to manage it but if I'm in a crunch over these next few hours, I'll let you know."

"How about lunch at least? My treat!"

"I may take you up on the offer. I owe you!"

"Anytime. I'll surprise you with something good. Maybe pick up a pie too and slam it in Jared's face!" They both laughed.

She tried to focus back in on her work but the lilies reminded her of Amy and her Mom and leaving Connecticut. She had wanted to stay longer, but also she didn't. Returning to work would ground her, and take her mind off the murder. Work had always distracted her, a habit of surroundings and situations. It took control when life seemed to spiral.

She placed the lilies next to some photos on her desk. One was of her and Zane after her college graduation. She sighed. She should text Zane to let him know she was back in California again so they could meet up. She needed to confront him about the real reason he was fired from Dad's hedge fund.

A knock at the door.

"Come in!"

Not wanting to lose focus, she kept her eyes on the computer screen.

"Hi, Madison."

The voice sounded sweet but it was a cover. It made her cringe, almost as much as Jared's did.

She looked up to see the beautiful, tall woman with long jet-black hair, tanned skin, and beautiful brown eyes standing before her. She wore her signature black-framed glasses, high-waisted pencil skirt, heels, and gray blouse.

"Hi, Tiffani. How are you?" Privately she was rolling her eyes, preparing herself for yet another passive-aggressive or fake show of support from someone she knew she could not trust.

Tiffani Hueger was an account manager who came over with Jared. Tiffani had the same position as Madison, but somehow, Jared convinced senior leadership to have her report directly to him. It was evident that Tiffani was a clear favorite of Jared's since she was always agreeable with him.

Madison had confided in her at a happy hour over the desire for more senior female leadership representation soon after she joined the company. She encouraged Tiffani to join the women's professional group as it would be a great chance to network and meet new people. She figured a possible shared interest in greater female representation would bond them.

Tiffani told Jared about their conversation. He pretended to care but no action came from it except for an awkward one-on-one meeting. She could still hear his sarcasm.

I hear you are concerned that there aren't enough female leaders here. Tell me about that.

Tiffani never joined the women's group, even though she expressed interest.

"Doing well. I know you were late to the beginning of Jared's meeting. I wanted to let you know Jared made us aware of a new presentation template to use in executive meetings going forward. I can show you on the shared drive where the template is located."

Tiffani directed her to the group's shared folder.

"It's this one right here."

Madison was surprised that Tiffani was offering help but feeling a bit apprehensive based on experience. She planned to run it by Bradley.

"Thanks for letting me know. I do appreciate it." Madison paused and thought she could use this as another opportunity to extend an olive branch. "How has your week been so far by the way? Everything been okay?"

"Yes, it's been busy as usual. Jared asked me to fly to Sydney next week to take part in a few meetings he cannot attend. I'm so excited!"

Ah. There it was. She wanted to brag about her upcoming trip.

"I'm happy for you. Well, I do need to get back to preparing for this presentation. Thanks again for letting me know about the new template."

"Anytime. Good luck today!"

The door slowly closed behind her. Madison let out a sigh of relief.

A few minutes later Bradley opened the door, carrying fish tacos and Mexican Coke.

"Hey, Bradley. Tiffani told me something about a new template for executive meetings. Did Jared mention this in the meeting this morning?"

"Oh yeah, he did remind the team to make sure to use the new template. I do have it. Want me to send you the link in the shared drive?"

Madison paused, feeling guilty now that it appeared Tiffani was telling the truth. Maybe she had turned a new leaf after all.

"No that's okay. I think I found it."

The Mexican Coke gave her the caffeine boost she needed to complete the presentation by the 3 p.m. deadline. After emailing Jared the slides, she also sent him a text message letting him know they were in his inbox.

He responded to the text message with a simple reply.

Received.

She did her best to shake off his cold response and focus her attention on giving an extraordinary presentation. For the next hour before the meeting, she prepared talking points and grabbed a cup of coffee before walking to the executive building across the parking lot.

4 p.m. finally arrived and the company's senior executive team gradually entered the conference room. Jared also entered and he immediately commanded the room, making crude jokes that they pretended to be amused by, but Madison could read the discomfort on their faces.

Tiffani sat across from Madison and both locked eyes. Why was she in this meeting and not Kristin?

After brief introductions, Jared announced that Madison would be presenting the latest update on her account first. She moved to the front of the room as her slides appeared on the screen. Beads of sweat started to form on her palms as she cleared her throat. All eyes were on her. Inside, she was terrified—she hated public speaking. Her voice started to tremble as she started to talk. She saw Tiffani giggle to herself. *You got this, Madison.*

Encouraging self-talk always helped. She gave a magnificent update on her account, an oral antiviral medication that just received FDA approval and was now preparing for market launch. She effortlessly breezed through the financial and schedule plans, providing the right level of detail while also showcasing her vibrant and warm personality along the way. It was evident that the executive team was engaged and impressed as she did a fabulous job of answering all questions.

As she confidently walked back to her seat, content with her ability to execute under such a tight time crunch, Jared stood up.

"Thanks, Madison, for the update. I did notice, however, you did not use the new template I had requested for this meeting. Please make sure you use that new template next time."

He then displayed Tiffani's presentation. Tiffani had purposely provided her with an outdated template. Madison reasoned it wasn't a catastrophe, but these snide actions were starting to compile. She would pull her aside after.

Jared continued, "Today, I will be having Tiffani provide the team overview. As we continue to grow, I am looking for a senior manager to be responsible for both domestic and international accounts. Tiffani will be traveling to Sydney next week for a customer meeting."

Did Kristin know about this? She was the account team manager. Most accounts under her responsibility were domestic, and it appeared now Jared had a promotion in the works for Tiffani to be one step above. She texted Kristin.

Kristin—why aren't you in this executive meeting?

She saw the bubbles float across the screen.

Jared wanted Tiffani to present today. I have a feeling she's going to be taking over global account management responsibility. I wouldn't be surprised if this means we end up reporting under her.

Madison's stomach felt like it had been punched a hundred times. She felt nauseous. Kristin deserved that role. Everyone loved her.

Thankfully, karma took over as Tiffani's presentation was lackluster at best. She mostly stumbled her way through, offering uninspired answers to the executives' questions. When pressed further on a few of her responses, there were numerous occasions in which she couldn't provide a follow-up, and Jared awkwardly had to come to her rescue. Kristin would have known the answers.

After the meeting ended, a few of the executives pulled Madison aside to congratulate her on a job well done. Madison saw Tiffani was still in the room.

"Hey, Tiffani, would you mind stepping out with me into the hallway? There's something I wanted to ask you."

Tiffani hesitantly followed behind.

Madison looked at her directly in the eyes. "Why on earth did you show me that template knowing it was not the updated one?"

Tiffani pressed her glasses to her face as they were beginning to slide off. "I'm sorry about that. I must have shown you the wrong one by accident. My bad!" This was followed by a mischievous grin. Madison could feel the sarcasm in her apology.

"I have to be frank. I don't believe you, especially given that you presented right after me with the correct template. How am I supposed to ever trust you when you have done other, equally shady, things to me in the past? This isn't the first time…"

Before she could continue, Tiffani interrupted, "Well it's not my fault you're paranoid! Again, it was an honest mistake. Looks like I won't be helping you anymore!"

Madison laughed to herself as Tiffani stormed off. She saw that Tiffani had found Jared at the end of the hallway, and both walked down the stairwell out of sight.

SAN DIEGO, CALIFORNIA

Monday, April 25, 2022
7 p.m.

Jared sat comfortably in his corner office overlooking the expansive atrium below, erratically responding to emails while planning his work for the next day.

He would often stay at the office late, doing what he could to avoid a home life that he wasn't particularly thrilled about. As he was in the middle of responding to another email in his usual condescending tone, he heard a polite knock on his office door. He was surprised—most people had gone home for the evening.

"Who is it?" Jared rudely snapped.

"Hi. Sorry to bother you, it's Kristin."

He questioned what she could possibly need this late. He enjoyed his alone time in the office at the end of a long day filled with constant meetings. Now that quiet time was being interrupted.

She entered his office cautiously. He hoped she wouldn't waste his time with small talk as he didn't have the energy to engage.

"I know it's getting late, but I was hoping to follow up on the request I made last week for Madison's promotion. You know Madison has been such a vital asset to this company for many years and she has demonstrated she can bring a product from development to market, creating the potential for millions in sales. She is more than deserving of a pay raise and title change. I hope you will approve this request?"

He thought to himself. Madison certainly wasn't his favorite employee, and he would prefer to give a promotion to Tiffani over her. But since Tiffani was his direct report and he was already eyeing her for the senior manager position, he knew he could accomplish that in his own time. And he did value Kristin, so perhaps he should follow through with her wishes.

"I'll approve it in the system tonight. It will also need VP approval. By the way, hopefully with this promotion Madison will do a better job at following direction. I was frustrated she couldn't even use the proper presentation template for the meeting today." He paused then continued, "Is there anything else I can help you with today? Hopefully not, it's getting late."

He could sense she was holding something back. She probably didn't like his last comment about Madison.

"That's all for tonight. I look forward to receiving your approval. I know the VP is out of the office starting early next week so I hope we can get this through by tomorrow."

Kristin quietly exited.

Quiet had finally returned. He didn't need any more distractions.

He read through a few more emails, and heard his phone vibrate. He had several missed text messages from his wife.

Where are you?

Get home now.

You're late again!

He turned off his computer. He would review the request for promotion tomorrow instead—it could wait another day. His wife was adamant he get home. He turned off the lights in his office and proceeded down the dark hallway toward the elevator. Most of the lights were off by now; a sole light in front of the elevator helped guide the way.

He heard what sounded like a bang behind him and turned around quickly to see what it could be. Nothing was there, only the faint glow of the moonlight from the outside windows.

The elevator light illuminated, and the doors opened. He stepped in toward the service doors in front of him which also opened, used to carry large items between the floors. Completely dark on the other side. He turned back around and glanced down at his watch. It was 8:30 p.m. He knew he would get a scolding from his wife for arriving home so late as this was becoming increasingly common. He felt frustrated that she was never satisfied. Did she not realize he was working hard to maintain the lifestyle she wanted?

He pressed the button for the first floor.

The elevator did not move nor did the doors close. He pressed the button again, but the doors still did not close.

"What the fuck!" he screamed.

Jared, now frustrated, hit the button repeatedly, and both sets of doors in the front and back eventually shut slowly.

"About fucking time!"

The elevator made its way down from the fourth floor.

Floor three.

Two.

Why did it feel like someone was in the elevator with him?

One.

Just as the front door opened, a hand from behind reached for the door close button, and pressed floor number four. The doors closed again, and Jared turned around to see who was standing behind him.

An individual dressed in black wearing a faceless mask stood before him. It looked like a hard gray shell and it was hard to see the eyes through the black filter. This person must have stepped inside the elevator from the service door earlier.

"Didn't realize it was already Halloween! You scared the crap out of me."

He then saw the glimmer of a large knife. Black blade. Brown leather handle.

"And with that thing, you could get fired so you better put it down, jackass."

Jared felt the knife penetrate his stomach. Blood gushed from the deep wound, soaking his white shirt and pouring onto the elevator floor. He fell to his knees as the elevator proceeded up.

The final sensation he felt as he knelt helplessly was the knife tearing into the front of his throat, a stab so deep that it pierced through to the back of his neck. Jared collapsed to the floor.

* * *

Kristin was in her third-floor office, finishing up the last of her emails before shutting down her computer. She looked for her purse which she'd misplaced, positive she had left it sitting on her office desk before going upstairs to speak with Jared. All she found was the silver chain necklace she had taken off earlier. She put it back on.

Normally, Kristin didn't stay at the office this late as her personal life was very important to her. She was especially grateful for her loving husband and twin toddler boys who she would sacrifice anything for. Tonight, she had stayed late only because she knew it was the best opportunity to approach Jared about the promotion request.

She shut off the lights in her office and walked to the women's restroom down the dark hallway. There was no sign of anyone else in the office. After opening the restroom door, she went into the first stall door and sat down. She reached for her phone and texted her husband.

Hi, honey. Sorry, I'm still at the office! I should be home in twenty minutes. Also, I can't find my purse. Luckily have a spare car key so will be able to get home. P.S. if the boys aren't already asleep, tell them I love them! I'll see you soon my love!

She then heard the bathroom door open. It was strange—she hadn't seen any of her co-workers in the building for at least an hour, other than Jared of course.

"Hello? Who's there?"

There was no response. Again, she called to inquire who it was.

Silence.

She finished in the stall, stood up slowly, and pulled down her skirt. She leaned over and peered through the crack in the stall door but could not see anyone, so she carefully opened it.

Unexpectedly, someone rushed in front of her carrying a large object. Kristin let out a scream and her phone dropped to the floor.

She looked up to see that it was only one of the female janitors carrying a broom. She sighed, and the janitor apologized profusely for startling her.

"Oh, ma'am, I am terribly sorry! I didn't realize anyone was in here. I had my headphones on playing music. Let me help you with your phone."

Kristin caught her breath. "Oh, no it's fine! It's just a work phone anyways. It can easily be replaced." She picked up her phone and tried to turn it on unsuccessfully. The front screen was completely shattered.

She walked toward the sink to wash her hands and politely chatted with the woman for a few moments.

"Listening to anything good by the way?"

"Romeo Santos. Well-known bachata musician."

"I love bachata. I studied abroad in Barcelona in college and took a bachata dance class there. Whenever I hear that style of music, it takes me to a tropical beach somewhere."

She said goodbye to the woman, wishing her a goodnight as she exited the restroom and walked toward the stairwell in the open glass atrium.

The open atrium in the building was a stunning modern design, with glass walls and ceilings that exposed all four floors. Each floor was connected by a winding spiral staircase. The first floor was comprised of a miniature botanical garden, café, meeting rooms, and open lounging space.

She paused while walking down and looked up toward the fourth floor. Jared's office light was on. She still had not received the approval from him in the system and was determined to push it through, especially since the VP was out of town next week. She had to talk to him again.

After arriving at the top of the staircase, she opened the glass door toward the hallway, with the light from his office guiding her down the dark hall. She nearly slipped on something wet on the floor but caught herself just in time.

She knocked and saw through the glass door that he was seated in his office chair, though it was turned around so she could only make out the top of his head.

There was no response, so she opened the door.

"Hey, Jared. Sorry to bother you again. It's Kristin. . ."

Silence. She reasoned he was probably annoyed with her at this point.

As she walked slowly toward the chair, she saw a thick red stain smeared on the gray carpet. Her heart started racing.

She reached out for the chair and turned it around slowly, letting out a loud scream as she saw what was before her—Jared's lifeless, rigid body. He appeared to have multiple stab wounds—a large one in the stomach, and another gaping hole in his throat. His eyes were still open and stared back at her.

Panic set in and she reached for his office phone to dial 9-1-1, knowing her own cell phone was broken. She was unable to dial out after multiple attempts. His office line had been disconnected.

She raced down the hallway, through the glass door in the atrium, and peered down.

Walking up the spiral staircase was someone who must have been the killer, wearing all black and a faceless mask. She saw the shimmer from the black knife they were wielding, likely the same knife that was used to kill Jared. It was apparent they were now coming for her.

With the stairway blocked as a potential exit, she raced toward the set of elevators. She repeatedly pressed the button as the killer briskly walked up the staircase. The elevator slowly ascended.

Floor two.

Three.

Four.

Finally, the elevator doors opened, and Kristin jumped in as the killer rounded the corner in her direction. After nearly slipping on the floors still wet with Jared's blood, she pressed the button for the basement level. The basement level could only be accessed by the one service elevator she was currently riding in.

The doors closed just in time before the killer could enter, and she breathed a momentary sigh of a relief as the elevator car made its way down to the basement.

The door eventually opened, and she sprinted out. Luckily, she was familiar with the basement, which they used as a storage area. The space was completely dark, but in the distance, she saw the dim glow of the exit sign. She stumbled past rows of boxes, crates, and delivery pallets toward it.

The exit door opened to the rear parking lot. Her car was in the front. She turned the corner to see if anybody was there. No one.

She sprinted along the west side of the building and looked around the corner towards the front parking lot and her Mercedes. Still clear.

Reaching for the spare key in her pocket, she ran toward her car, being careful not to make any loud sounds. Thankfully, she reached the door and jumped into the driver's seat, immediately locking it. After catching her breath, she started the car and raced through the parking lot toward the exit gate. The iron gate, though normally open during business hours, was now closed.

She noticed her missing purse laying on the passenger seat floor—the same purse that had her other car key inside. There's no way she left it there.

Kristin's eyes flicked to the rearview mirror where the gray mask appeared. Dark, soulless eyes.

Before she could let out a scream, the killer reached forward, wrapped the seatbelt around her neck, and began to strangle her.

She desperately tried to reach for her purse, and finally got a hold of it. Her hands found the bottle of pepper spray inside, something she'd carried since college. Just as she was slowly fading out of consciousness, she sprayed it in the direction of the killer, who struggled and released the seatbelt.

She ran out of the car, toward the gate, and entered the code on the keypad. It opened slowly from left to right, wobbling against the track, letting out a loud screeching sound. Just when there was enough of an opening, she started to step through.

Unfortunately, with only one foot through to the other side, her necklace caught on the gate rail. At first, she tried to pull on the necklace hoping it would break, but the silver chains were too thick.

The killer exited the car and walked to the gate keypad. They pressed a red emergency close button and watched Kristin struggle as the gate closed on her.

The thick iron inched closer and closer as she attempted to unclasp her necklace. She tried desperately to locate the clasp but was unsuccessful. Her lower body stepped out of the way of the moving gate during the struggle, but her head was still directly in its path.

As the heavy gate contacted her head, she let out a terrifying scream. The gate violently jolted and sparked as her head obstructed its closing. Blood poured from her mouth and eye sockets. After her skull cracked, her body went limp.

8

A line of police cars and media outlets blocked the front gate at 7:30 a.m. Officers approached arriving employees, seemingly as confused as Madison was. She pulled forward and rolled down the driver's window as an officer walked toward her.

"Hi, Officer. Good morning. I work here. What happened? Are they not letting cars in right now?"

The officer knelt and made eye contact. "Hi, ma'am. I believe a companywide email was sent moments ago. All employees should work from home today until further instructions are provided by the company."

"What happened?"

"It's a crime scene, ma'am. Please refer to your company email."

She stared back at the officer with a blank expression. Today was supposed to be a good day, a productive day. She'd arrived especially early.

"Thanks for letting me know."

She drove toward the traffic light on the corner and immediately instructed her car's voice control system to call Bradley.

"Hey, Madison. I'm about ten minutes away from work. Are you at the office yet?"

She paused. "You are not going to believe it, but they have our entire work campus completely blocked off. Something happened. The officer wouldn't say what but it must be bad."

Bradley gasped. "What? Are you serious?"

"Apparently we're all supposed to work remotely today. Do you want to meet at the coffee shop on Liberty Avenue and we can figure things out from there? Guess they sent a companywide email out about the situation, but I have yet to read it."

"Yes, let's do it. This is crazy! I'll see you in ten minutes."

She hung up and turned the corner. While driving, all she could think about what possibly could have happened. She instructed the car's voice control to call Kristin.

The phone rang, but there was no response. She called again, but Kristin's phone kept ringing before going to voicemail. A sense of dread took over—Kristin always picked up her calls. And if she was unavailable, she would usually text right away. There was no text this time. Madison drove for a few more minutes before finally reaching the coffee shop parking lot.

Knowing Bradley was still a few minutes away, she reached for her work email and scrolled through her unread messages. Toward the top, she saw the company email that had been sent thirty minutes earlier. She anxiously opened it.

From: Chris Brenton
Sent: Tuesday, April 26, 2022 7:15 a.m.
Subject: Incident On Campus Last Night

Dear employees,
There was an incident on campus last night in Building # 1 and authorities have identified it as a crime scene. While further details can't be shared at this time, we are currently instructing all employees in all buildings on campus to work remotely until further notice. As soon as we have more information available, we will send a follow-up email with an update. We thank you for your patience.

Please reach out to your HR contact if you have any immediate concerns or questions.
Sincerely,
Chris Brenton
CEO

What could have happened?

Suddenly, someone was banging loudly on Madison's car door. She jumped in her seat, then looked outside to see it was Bradley. Relieved, she got out and embraced her friend, and they walked inside the coffee shop.

"Bradley, did you read the email? They aren't releasing any details of what happened yet."

"I know. Only saying it's a crime scene."

"I wonder what type of crime scene?"

"Well, when I hear crime scene, I immediately think murder."

"No way! At work? I really hope not."

"Hopefully they send an update later today."

After ordering, they walked toward the counter to pick up their coffee. Madison quickly noticed that Tiffani was inside the coffee shop as well, the last person she wanted to see. She avoided making eye contact, but it was too late; Tiffani was already approaching.

"Good morning. I'm sure you guys heard there was an incident at work last night?"

Madison didn't want to have this conversation with her right now.

"Yeah, we read the email but not much information was provided. Have you heard any more details?"

Tiffani reached for her cup of coffee in sync with it appearing on the counter in front of her. She lowered her voice.

"Do you promise not to disclose what I'm about to tell you?"

Madison and Bradley looked at each other and nodded in agreement.

Tiffani continued, "I found out Jared was murdered last night. As you are aware, I was very close with him, equally as close with his wife Margaret. I spoke with Margaret early this morning and she gave me some details which haven't been disclosed yet. Apparently, Jared was found stabbed to death in his office and another employee was also killed. Margaret doesn't know who though. The police are reviewing security camera footage from the building, but they haven't named any official suspects yet."

Jared was murdered? Madison was in disbelief. She could barely speak.

Bradley stepped in and responded to Tiffani.

"Stabbed to death? That is horrible! I feel bad for his wife. And you said another employee was also killed?"

"Yes, but I don't know who it was. Wish I had the inside scoop on that. Hopefully, I can find something out."

Madison remembered Kristin hadn't picked up her call earlier. She became anxious. She reached for her phone. Kristin had not texted or called back.

"Has anyone heard from Kristin today?"

Bradley and Tiffani both shook their heads.

Madison sent Kristin a text. There had to be a perfectly good explanation why she hadn't responded yet.

Hey—please call me when you get this. I'm worried about you.

Madison continued, "Tiffani, do you have any idea who would want Jared dead? I know he wasn't the nicest person to a lot of people at work, but that's no reason for murder."

"Well, I know you weren't always the biggest fan of him, and that there was sometimes conflict between you two. Maybe you are aware of someone who would target him?"

There it was. The cunning and calculating side of Tiffani; the side that Madison too often witnessed, but others failed to recognize as she was an expert at appearing friendly. Was Tiffani really implying that Madison knew someone who would want to kill Jared?

After catching her breath, she responded.

"Well, Jared and I certainly did have our disagreements, but nothing that would warrant this type of tragic situation. And of course, I'm not aware of anyone that would want to hurt him. Are you?"

Bradley, always having his friend's back, replied, "Instead of sneakily pointing fingers, how about you show some compassion? I can't believe this is what you want to talk about. Seriously back the fuck off."

Tiffani pressed her black-framed glasses to her face and appeared perplexed. Probably plotting a witty reply, but ultimately, she failed to say anything. She just grimaced at them then walked off with her skinny vanilla latte in hand.

"She's a real piece of work, isn't she?"

"Not my favorite that's for sure. But at least we know a little more about what happened last night. I'm going to head home. Keep me posted if you hear anything else."

"I will. Drive home safe!"

She worked from home the rest of the day and asked some of her colleagues if they had heard from Kristin. No one had. Kristin was offline on Slack. Madison constantly refreshed her email to see if there was another company-wide update. 5 p.m. and still no email from Chris.

She brought her work phone to the gym with her. Thirty minutes in Bradley texted her.

Check your work email now. Call me after.

Madison jumped off the treadmill and stepped outside. A cold breeze brushed against her skin. She pulled out her work phone and refreshed her email. A new message from Chris Brenton appeared.

From: Chris Brenton
Sent: Tuesday, April 26, 2022 7:00 p.m.
Subject: Incident On Campus Last Night (UPDATE)

Dear employees,
We wanted to share an update regarding the email we sent earlier today regarding the incident on campus last night.

It is with great sadness that I share with you the loss of two of our employees, Jared Demange and Kristin Tate, last night due to an unfortunate crime. While specific details aren't being released at this time, Jared and Kristin both were found deceased on campus late yesterday evening.

We will continue to keep all employees apprised of the latest information we receive from law enforcement and the ongoing investigation into their deaths. We don't believe there is an immediate threat to other employees, but out of an abundance of caution, we are currently instructing all employees to continue to work remotely. The safety of our employees will always be our number one priority.

Kristin Tate had been with the company for over ten years, most recently leading our account management team. She will be remembered for her radiant personality and positive, upbeat attitude, someone who was always willing to lend a helping hand to others.

Jared Demange had been with the company for two years, serving as director of our account management and technical teams. He will be remembered for helping to transform and expand the business into what it is today—a biotech firm with a global market share.

Kristin and Jared will be profoundly missed, and I'm sure both have impacted many of you personally and professionally.

The company is working with their loved ones on how we can best support them during this difficult period. At this time of great loss, it is important that we continue to support one another. Should you *need additional assistance, please reach out to your HR representative.*

We do not yet have details yet on services, however, once we have more information, we will be sure to share it with the team as appropriate. Our deepest condolences go out to Kristin and Jared's family, friends, and co-workers.
Sincerely,
Chris Brenton
CEO

Madison's heart sank and tears flowed down her cheeks. She reread the email a couple more times, as if that might change the names. Her worst fears were now a reality—Kristin was the other employee killed last night.

9

News broke the next day that Jared and Kristin had been murdered.

Madison was in shock that something so violent could have happened at her workplace, somewhere she should have felt safe. Detectives were interviewing all their immediate co-workers over that week and the weekend. Her interview was scheduled for Saturday afternoon.

Losing Dad earlier in the year was hard enough. Having to cope with Amy and Kristin's sudden deaths was devastating. Amy's killer still had not been identified, and Madison was perplexed by who would want Kristin and Jared dead. Could it be a disgruntled co-worker? But everyone loved Kristin. And surely no one would go to the extreme of killing Jared just because he was difficult to work with?

A day after it was made public that Jared and Kristin were murdered, Madison received a text from Paxton, the tall, mysterious man she'd met at the club the same night Amy was murdered. He wanted to go on a date with her Friday. She messaged Bradley and Jessica.

Paxton, the guy I met at the club, wants to go on a date tomorrow. I can't do it with everything that has been happening.

Jessica responded.

I get it. It's been a horrible year for you. But, maybe getting out would do you good? Get your mind off things and help you return to some sense of normalcy. I say go and give it a shot. I hope to see you at the dance studio next week.

Bradley's response followed.

You owe it to yourself to find love again. A sexy guy like Paxton doesn't come around often. If you don't go, I will.

Bradley always knew the right thing to say to make her laugh. Her initial reaction was not to accept the invite but as the day progressed, she recognized doing something for herself wouldn't hurt. Since she was also working remotely all week, she felt isolated in her apartment and needed to get out. She texted Paxton back.

Hey Paxton. I'm down to meet tomorrow. Any places in mind?

She saw the bubbles appear in their text conversation.

I've made a reservation at that new rooftop sushi restaurant, Luma, at 8 p.m. Looking forward to it!

While she was on her way to the restaurant the next day, Zane also texted her.

In town for a work conference at the San Diego convention center until tomorrow. Want to meet up for a drink tonight? You could use one after this week. I'm so sorry again about what happened to your co-workers.

Madison responded.

Zane, I unfortunately already have plans. Grabbing a drink with a friend at Luma. Still feeling down but need to get out to take my mind off things. Let's hang out soon. We need to talk.

She still had to confront him about the embezzlement scheme. Better to do it in person.

She arrived at the rooftop sushi restaurant fifteen minutes late for her date. Her red cocktail dress nearly got caught in the elevator door as she jumped in at the last minute with a handful of other guests. Once reaching the twentieth floor, she was greeted by a hostess in the open-air restaurant who led her to the table where Paxton was sitting.

A nervous energy filled her; she was curious to learn more about Paxton, though she certainly wasn't in a rush to enter another relationship so soon on the heels of her breakup. She felt conflicted—companionship brought happiness in many ways, but independence was something she knew she needed. Especially at this point in her life when she was experiencing so much tragedy and needed time to grieve on her own.

As she walked toward the table, she noticed the vibrant colors of her surroundings. It contrasted with her grief. The restaurant had a modern, clean design with splashes of bright color in the artwork and décor, including yellow, orange, blue, red, and purple. Artsy and vibrant murals of geishas and buddhas adorned the space. Japanese plants surrounded the tables and lounge areas, which included bamboo and a fake cherry tree in full bloom. An ornate black-and-white tile mosaic floor grounded the space.

The sky above was now dark and chill ambient house music filled the area. The sound was not overwhelming but fit the decidedly cool and contemporary vibe of the venue. On a normal night, this setting would be right up Madison's alley. Tonight, though she looked the part, no one could imagine the pain she was feeling inside.

Once she laid eyes on Paxton, she instantly remembered why she'd been so attracted in the first place. He stood up to greet her, and she realized she'd forgotten how tall he was as he gave her a warm hug and kiss on the cheek. His soft, sensual lips were just as gentle as she remembered. She took comfort in the warm embrace he gave her.

"Paxton, I am so sorry I'm late. My Uber was slow in picking me up."

"Don't worry at all. I was a little late myself due to a client meeting that ran over. Don't sweat it. All that matters is that you're here now. By the way, it is a little chilly up here. Can I offer you my jacket? Or I can have the waiter come by to turn on one of the heaters for us?"

He immediately flagged a waiter to turn on the heater directly above their table.

"By the way, Madison, you look absolutely stunning."

He looked even more handsome than she remembered. He was wearing a casual gray fitted suit with a white shirt underneath. Part of the shirt was unbuttoned, showing off his perfectly trimmed chest hair and defined pectorals. His hair was clean-cut and styled just like it had been the night she had met him.

She appreciated his charm and charisma. Though their first interaction was brief, these traits had come across the night they met. Part of her believed it was almost too good to be true. She also didn't expect to meet someone like him so soon after breaking up with Kyle. She knew it was too soon, especially with everything that had transpired. But she wanted to give it a chance.

"Sorry by the way if I'm too dressed up. I had a trial downtown today. Removed my tie so I didn't look too formal."

She remembered him mentioning he was a lawyer.

He continued, "So, how has your week been so far? Anything eventful happen?"

If only Paxton knew. Madison froze. She didn't know how to

respond. She couldn't dump everything on him right away. But she didn't want to dismiss everything that had happened.

"I'll be completely honest. It has been a difficult week. A difficult year really. I've suffered some personal losses. I'd prefer not to talk about it too much tonight."

He looked concerned. He grabbed her hand from across the table and caressed it.

"I'm so sorry to hear. I completely understand if you don't want to talk about it. Losing someone you love is painful. I'm here if you ever need someone to talk to."

She felt a sense of relief. That's all she needed to hear. Someone who acknowledged her feelings but also respected her desire for privacy.

They eventually ordered sake, followed by a wide array of appetizers and specialty sushi rolls. His manners shined through, allowing her to always order first while ensuring she was happy and comfortable. When the food finally did come out from the kitchen, the presentation was like a piece of colorful artwork, so beautiful that Madison felt guilty eating it. The explosion of taste in her mouth was complex and flavorful enough to overcome that guilt.

As the night progressed, she became more relaxed and embraced the ambiance, the conversation, and the wonderfully handsome date she was with. She felt guilty for stepping out of her shell and enjoying herself, even if it was short-lived. The sake also helped.

After finishing their dinner, they both ordered desserts. While waiting for them to arrive, she departed for the restroom with her purse in hand. After a quick look-over in the bathroom mirror, she re-applied her red lipstick carefully. She also splashed herself with a spritz of perfume, a scent that was floral with hints of rose and jasmine as well as a touch of vanilla.

Madison originally wasn't planning on inviting Paxton back to her apartment but based on how the night was transpiring, she was open to the idea. She felt comfortable and safe with him. She was enjoying the flirtation. Though she hadn't fully opened up, she saw potential to express her more vulnerable side.

Upon returning to the table, she saw the dessert along with new tableware had arrived. They'd both ordered ice cream, but this was not any ordinary ice cream. It was a mix of vanilla and green tea swirled together in the shape of a sushi roll. The outside was tempura battered and drizzled with chocolate sauce and coconut shavings.

"This looks delicious. I hope you enjoy it," Paxton smiled.

She smiled back at him before reaching for her new napkin and set of silverware that had been placed while she was in the restroom. As she unrolled her napkin, something fell out onto the floor just below her. Paxton was distracted, already devouring his plate of ice cream. She looked down and saw that it looked like several pieces of paper.

Three photos.

One was of Amy Carlisle from her high school yearbook. The second and third were headshots of Kristin Tate and Jared Demange from the company's yearbook last year. All three had large red cross marks in the shape of the letter X across their faces.

Fear and disbelief overtook her. She placed the photos on the table in front of her. Paxton was still gorging on the ice cream in front of him, completely distracted.

She sat stock-still, perplexed. Someone was clearly connecting Amy's death to Kristin and Jared. But Amy had never met Jared or Kristin. The only thing that tied them together was that Madison knew all of them.

Madison looked toward Paxton and gazed at him as he consumed his dessert like a starving animal. She wondered if he was involved at all in planting the photos. Or, even worse, in the murders. He couldn't have killed Amy because Madison met him the weekend she was killed. Maybe there were two killers conspiring together?

Her gut reaction was that he couldn't be involved—what would be the motive? It was strange though that all these murders started soon after meeting him. Who else possibly could have planted these photos? Paxton would have had the perfect opportunity to do it while she was in the restroom.

She had to think of an excuse to make a quick exit from her date.

"Hey, I just got a text from my brother who is in town. He got into a car accident. He is okay but was admitted to the hospital as a precaution. I'm sorry but I have to go. Let me pay for the meal."

Hopefully he would buy her story.

"Hope everything is okay! And you don't have to pay. This is my treat. I drove here—let me take you to the hospital."

"No, I couldn't ask you to do that. I can just Uber home and drive from there. I wish I could stay but I must go now."

Now was the time to make a swift exit. She stood up from her chair. He unexpectedly grabbed a hold of her arm. His grip was tight.

"Madison, I insist on taking you. It really isn't an issue. Let me pay and then we can go together."

He wouldn't let go of her arm. She tried to wiggle away but his grip seemed to tighten.

"Please let go."

"I insist. I can't leave you alone."

He still didn't release her. Maybe Paxton *was* somehow involved? The aggression was suspicious, and she felt increasingly fearful. She saw a silver knife still lying on the table. She contemplated grabbing it.

She noticed he also caught her staring at it.

"Paxton, let go of me!" she screamed.

"I'm sorry, I was just worried about you." He finally released her arm.

"I—I…don't give me that shit!" she yelled. She felt relieved now that he didn't have a hold of her.

The surrounding tables could sense something was wrong and glanced over.

Madison grabbed the photos and walked away, noticing the stares of the other diners around her.

As she exited, she briefly glanced back in Paxton's direction. She could hear him say something to the guests that were seated at the table next to them.

"First date." He smiled along with the other guests.

Once outside, Madison felt the phone in her purse vibrate. It was Dawn.

"Hey, Dawn." She stopped to catch her breath.

"You okay? Just wanted to check in on you."

"Not really. Two of my co-workers were murdered this week. Their names were Jared and Kristin."

"What? I'm so sorry. Was it another person from your company who did it?"

"They don't know yet. But I was just out on a date and found three photos. One of Amy from our high school yearbook. The other two were of Jared and Kristin from my company's yearbook. Each photo had an X over their faces."

"Is someone suggesting that they are somehow connected?"

"I don't know."

"Wait, did you say all the photos were from a *yearbook*?"

"Yeah."

There was silence on the phone for several seconds.

"Dawn, you still there?"

"Yes. Just thinking. Didn't you also receive a note saying *hot tub* when you were on your way back home in the train?"

"Yes…"

"Remember that prank we played on your brother at the Cape house after finding the love note to Amy in her yearbook? Weren't we outside your basement and we eventually led Zane into the hot tub after he took off his clothes?"

"Now that I think about it…yes, we did. What are you trying to say?"

"I think you know."

"Shit. Zane's in town too. Let me call you back."

"Okay, be safe. Call me anytime."

Madison leaned against the building outside and placed her hands to her face. She felt paralyzed. Could it be Zane? Tomorrow's interview with the detectives about Jared and Kristin would be the perfect opportunity to bring up her suspicions. But first, she had to confront Zane. She needed answers.

10

She texted Zane at 6 a.m. the next morning.

Hey—headed to my gym downtown in 30 minutes. It's near the convention center. Want to meet for a workout before your conference?

He responded minutes later. *Sure. Text me the address.*

Thirty minutes later she was waiting outside the gym. Her place of strength. She saw him turn the corner and walk in her direction. They hugged.

"Well, this was convenient. My hotel's right around the block."

"Glad you could meet up."

They opened the door and checked in at the front desk. Zane would use a guest pass today. Glass windows surrounded them as they ascended the LED-lit stairs.

"How do you feel about working out on the rooftop turf area? Tons of weights there too."

Zane nodded and once they reached the second floor, Madison led him to a set of glass doors at the rear.

"Fancy gym. The one I go to is nothing like this."

She gave a fake smile. She had to make him feel comfortable so he wouldn't hold back any information. Once outside, they walked to a bench in the corner of the grass turf. Beautiful views in the distance of the ballpark and the bay as it shimmered in the early morning sunlight.

"So, I've been trying to use weights more," she told him. "Want to build more strength. Shall we try dumbbell chest presses?"

"Wow, I'm impressed, sis. Didn't realize you had it in you. I'm down. I'll spot you first."

She grabbed two thirty-pound dumbbells and laid back against the bench. She completed all twelve reps without assistance from her brother.

"Your turn. Show me what you got." He grabbed two fifty-pound dumbbells and did his first set with ease. Now was the moment to say something. With adrenaline pumping, hopefully he would speak.

"Why didn't you ever tell me the real reason you were fired from Dad's company?"

He sat up on the bench and looked her in the eye. "Well, this is random. I thought you knew. It was all over some stolen money."

"Don't play dumb with me. It's more than that. You embezzled investor funds. Thousands of dollars."

"How did you find out?"

"When I was home. Found some of Dad's old work emails. Why didn't you tell me? I thought we told each other everything."

"I was embarrassed, okay! I messed up. Bad. And I know that. I didn't want you thinking any different of me."

Now was the time to mention the photos.

"The killer left me a message last night while I was on a date."

"What was it?"

"A photo of Amy from her high school yearbook. Photos of my dead co-workers Kristin and Jared from my company's yearbook. All with an X over their faces."

"So are their deaths somehow connected?"

"I also received a note when I traveled back home for Amy's funeral. It said *hot tub*."

"Well, that's odd."

"I thought so too. But remember that prank me, Amy, and Dawn played on you the summer before college? It was in the hot tub at the Cape and you confessed your love for Amy in her yearbook. See a connection?"

He appeared baffled. "Wait are you saying I had something to do with this?"

"I just find it odd, that's all. You would never..." *Should I say kill?* "...do anything...to hurt anyone as revenge, right?"

"You mean like murder? Madison, you're sounding crazy right now. I'm your brother."

"I had to ask. I know you were in New York City for a business trip. Not too far of a drive to Westport..."

"So, you really think I killed Amy?" He looked mad and disappointed all at once. Was it an act?

"I—I hope not..."

He stood up from the bench and reached for his phone in his pocket. He started scrolling through it.

"Well, how did I magically kill Amy while I was on a flight to New York?" He handed his phone to her. "Here, take a look."

She looked at the screen. An email confirmation of his flight itinerary.

Departure: LAX Friday, April 1, 2022 10 p.m.
Arrival: JFK Saturday, April 2, 2022 6 a.m.

A red-eye flight. Amy was killed around midnight. He couldn't have been there even if the flight arrived a little earlier than scheduled. She felt guilty. Maybe she was too quick to assume the worst.

"Plus, the messages you received could mean anything. Wasn't Amy murdered in a hot tub? Could those three photos have been planted there just so you knew the murders were connected? There could be any number of reasons. But I didn't do this to seek revenge for a prank. I'm hurt in all honesty. I'm going to use the restroom. I'll be right back."

He stepped inside the building.

Madison was starting to doubt her reasoning. She then remembered Zane's social media post the weekend of Amy's murder. She didn't remember the time stamp. She pulled out her phone and went to Zane's Facebook page.

She scrolled down and found it. *6:30 a.m.* She read the caption. "Just landed in New York City!" The photo matched Zane's timeline of events. She felt even worse.

He returned outside. "Let's forget this conversation. Your turn." He pointed to the bench. "Not sure if you trust your serial killer brother though."

"Zane—I, I'm sorry. I just wanted to be sure. I believe you."

A seed of doubt remained but he had a solid alibi the night of Amy's murder. She lifted the thirty-pound dumbbells and started her second set as Zane spotted behind her. They seemed heavier this time. She started to struggle on the eighth rep. She counted out loud.

Eight. Nine. Ten.

By ten her arms were trembling.

Eleven.

She started to lift but her arms buckled. She felt a set of arms reach from behind to guide her up.

"Twelve," she screamed out. Zane guided her hands back down before she dropped the weights on the turf.

"See, I always have your back. I need you to have mine."

She had her interview coming up that afternoon with the detectives. She thought about how bad she would feel if she mentioned Zane as a possible suspect and he ended up not being involved in any of it. She decided for now she would trust her brother and not say anything.

11

Madison strolled the boardwalk with Jessica along Mission Beach and toward The Heat.

This afternoon, Jessica decided they needed to dance. Maybe some salsa. *It's Cinco de Mayo, Madison,* she'd texted. *Feel your inner chica.* The sun was low in the sky and the surfers were catching the last waves. Beach volleyballers finished their sets. The boardwalk bars pounded reggaeton while partygoers danced, sloshing margaritas on each other. Jessica grinned and took Madison's hand then stepped out and swayed her hips. "Come on."

The sudden burst of energy took Madison off guard. She gave a thin smile and a sad swish of the hips.

"Well, that won't do." Jessica smacked her on the butt. "I know you have more than that."

"I'm trying."

They walked in silence for a few steps. "How did the interview with detectives go on Saturday? You haven't said anything yet." Silence. "I'm here for you. You know that, right?"

"I know." She smiled at her friend and took a deep breath. "It was supposed to be about Jared and Kristin. Ended up talking about Paxton." She rolled her shoulders and head a little, trying to loosen the tension lodged in her neck. "They knew about Amy and asked for the photos. It all seems connected, right?"

"What did you say about Paxton?"

"He was one of the people who could have planted them there."

"That's insane. The situation, not you." She took Madison's hand and squeezed it gently. "I'm so sorry you're going through all this."

"The killer had to have planted them on my date. They were taken from Jared and Kristin's yearbook after the murders."

"How do you know they were taken after?"

"Grapevine."

"Tiffani?"

Madison nodded and rolled her eyes.

"Too bad it wasn't her."

"Jessica!"

"Just saying the obvious."

"They brought Paxton in for questioning. Kept him a few hours but cleared him. Insufficient evidence."

"Insufficient—?"

"Solid alibi. He wasn't even in the vicinity when the murders happened."

"But you still suspect him?"

"Honestly, I don't know what to think. I guess anyone could have planted the photos."

Madison decided not to tell Jessica about her initial suspicion of Zane since she now believed it wasn't him. He had a solid alibi and she didn't want to get him into any trouble.

"Yeah, it's totally possible someone else did it while the waitstaff or Paxton weren't looking. Did the detectives say anything else?"

"They'll keep me updated and they've already contacted Connecticut authorities."

"There's a connection? Like a serial killer?"

Madison bit at her bottom lip. The crease between her brows grew deeper. "Maybe."

"But they're all people you know. Amy, Kristin, Jared—" They both went silent. Jessica took a deep breath. "Do they suspect you?"

"They didn't say that." Her eyes swelled with tears. "I don't know how much more of this I can take, Jess. I'm really scared."

"Hey, it's okay. It's all going to be okay. They'll find out who it is and catch her—"

"Who says it's a her?"

"I wasn't going to say anything, but I really didn't like Jared…"

"Very funny."

"Anything to get you to smile." Jessica gave a deep swish of the hips and drew her friend into her arms. "Come on. Let's get you to the studio."

They stepped off the boardwalk and through The Heat's main door and climbed the flight of stairs to the second-floor dance studio. The last group class was ending and twenty or so dancers headed down the stairs. The setting sun streamed through the floor-to-ceiling windows, a few of them open, letting in the cool ocean breeze.

"I'll lock up," Jessica said to the instructor as she closed the door behind her.

Bradley was already in the studio, warming up and blasting 'Toxic'.

"Britney Spears, again, Bradley?" Jessica shouted.

"Only my favorite, of course."

Madison laughed.

He continued to dance a choreographed set, mostly to impress his friends with the latest moves he had been practicing for weeks. They cheered him on. Jessica was the most seasoned dancer of the three, however, Bradley and Madison's techniques had improved over the years under her guidance.

"Okay, enough of me. Let's put on a classic '80s Janet Jackson song that we all know and love!"

Bradley rushed to the corner sound system, queuing up 'What Have You Done For Me Lately.'

All three friends positioned themselves in front of the mirrors lining the wall and counted—five, six, seven, eight. A rush of energy surged through their bodies as the music pulsated throughout the room. They danced with tremendous power, complete with sharp shoulder shrugs, quick head bops, and expressive arm and hip movements as they slid across the dancefloor.

They pretended they were putting on a show for a large audience, something the three of them had never done together before. The choreography and quality of their routine were professional enough that they could easily do well in any dance competition. Jessica had brought up the idea a few times to her friends before, but nothing ever materialized; for now, they were content with performing amongst themselves, all in good fun.

They continued for another hour or so until Madison grew tired, ready to wind down.

"How about we head to Ocean Bar for a few Cinco de Mayo drinks?" Jessica suggested.

Madison replied, "Thank you, both. I love you. This really helped. But I think I'm done for the night."

"Nonsense. You're coming with us." Bradley set his hands on his hips and gave Madison *the stare*. There was no defense against *the stare*.

Jessica raised her brows and put up her hands. "Looks like we're going out."

Jessica, whose parents immigrated to the United States from Mexico, never understood why Americans were so keen on celebrating Cinco de Mayo. She found it amusing as it was rarely celebrated in her native country. Regardless, she was never one to turn down a few margaritas.

"Fine!" Madison exclaimed.

"But don't you guys want to shower and change first?" Bradley asked.

Madison and Jessica looked at each other. They did not bring a change of clothes or make-up. That wouldn't stop them from grabbing drinks—they weren't looking to meet anyone new anyway.

Bradley continued, "You guys go. I'm drenched in sweat! I'm going to shower in the locker room, change, then meet you."

"Always the woman in the group!" Madison joked.

"Hey, there may be some curious surfer boys that are up for a little late-night fun, so I have to be fresh, if you know what I mean."

Jessica and Madison looked at each other and laughed. Bradley was the flirtatious type and used his undeniable charm and good looks to woo all types of men, even straight ones who were open to exploring.

"All right, well, don't take too long, Bradley. Here are the keys to the studio. Please lock up. Text us when you're on your way!"

Madison and Jessica quickly changed shirts, packed their belongings into their purses, and proceeded down the stairwell toward the exit.

SAN DIEGO, CALIFORNIA

Thursday, May 5, 2022
8:30 p.m.

Bradley walked into the men's locker room.
It was small, with a single row of lockers and benches on one wall and a few shower stalls on the other. He grabbed a towel from one of the racks and put his belongings, including the keys Jessica handed him, in a locker. He took off his sweatpants and tank top and turned to look in the mirror. He worked tirelessly on his chest and abdomen and was looking toned and chiseled. He pinched at his waist and noticed a little more give than usual. It would be salads and protein for a week.

He wrapped the towel around his waist and made his way toward the shower with his phone in his hand. He turned on the water and held a hand in the stream, waiting for it to warm.

After a few seconds, he hung his towel on the hanger beside the shower curtain and propped his phone on the little chair. Janet Jackson had put him in the mood for more '80s music. Something sensual. He pushed play. The power chords and heavy percussion of 'Shout' by Tears for Fears played through the locker room.

The water was perfect, both cooling and relaxing. He contemplated a moment of self-pleasure but resisted. Better save it for any possible fun later. He washed his hair, face, and body, singing along with the song.

A loud thud sounded, then the locker room went dark. Completely dark. He pulled his right hand up but couldn't see it.

"Hello? Jessica? Madison? Is that you?"

No response.

"This isn't funny. I know it's you. I'm completely naked in here and can't see so would really appreciate it if you could turn the lights back on!"

Still no response.

He reached outside the shower and flailed a little to find his towel. After drying off and wrapping the towel around his waist, he whipped back the shower curtain, certain Jessica would be standing there, waiting for him to blindly walk into her. He put a hand out and felt left and right, but no one was there.

Then a soft light shone from the right where the locker room door had swayed open and closed, again. Must have been the ocean breeze. He'd forgotten to close the studio windows. He felt his way to the light switch, turned on the overheads, then switched off the music. It was definitely them. Jessica more than Madison. Jessica had an evil streak.

Hate you both! He group-texted.

He opened the door and peered into the dark studio. The towel slipped a little and he cinched it up, pulled it tighter around his waist. "Madison and Jessica, come out now, or I can guarantee that I will steal whatever men you are flirting with tonight!"

Silence.

He reached for the light switch on the studio wall but it wouldn't turn on. Frustrated, he started to turn back into the locker room when the moonlight cast onto the mirrors. Large red handwriting.

TONIGHT'S YOUR NIGHT TO DIE PRETTY BOY!

Jessica could be cutting but not even she would write that.

He had been bullied and harassed in high school when he first came out. He wouldn't start an altercation but he was fierce and didn't shy from defending himself either. A few kids teased him and picked fights but he was tall and strong and usually won. Bullies eventually learned not to bother him.

Who would write such a threatening message? He had very few enemies or even people that judged him. Kristin and Jared and Amy flashed before him and he touched the mirror. Red lipstick.

He looked around the moonlit studio. No sign of anyone. Time to get dressed and go. He walked back into the men's locker room and changed into jeans and a T-shirt. He would find the girls and report the incident. No party tonight. He turned to the mirror and saw some of the red lipstick had smeared on the white T-shirt. *Damn.*

He headed to the sink, turned on the faucet, and soaped his hands, then bent over to rinse his face when a noise sounded behind him. He popped up to the mirror to see what it was but his eyes were stinging from some soap he'd neglected to rinse. He bent over again when the noise sounded a second time.

He quickly splashed water into his eyes and stood up. To his horror, in the mirror, a figure dressed in black and wearing a gray mask stood behind him. No face. Only two black holes for eyes. The figure slowly raised a knife above his head. Looked like some sort of hunting or fighting knife with its long black blade.

Bradley ducked to the right as the killer brought the knife down, narrowly missing him. The killer lost balance from the momentum and Bradley attacked, both falling and struggling on the floor. Bradley grappled for the knife but the killer regained control and slashed his arm.

Bradley jumped up and ran out of the locker room door toward the exit but the door wouldn't open. He pulled and kicked at the door, but it was locked. Someone must have taken the keys. The killer fast approached and Bradley ran to the windows that only partially opened. Impossible for him to open completely but maybe he could crash through. He frantically searched the studio for a heavy object to break the glass. There was a metal chair in the corner. He hurled it at the window but the glass didn't break. His last hope was to attract attention on the boardwalk below for help.

Below on the boardwalk were four runners with headphones on. Behind them strolled a group of intoxicated Cinco de Mayo partiers blasting Latin music from a large speaker. He yelled and pounded hard on the glass. Neither the runners nor the partiers heard him through the noise.

He turned and started toward the locker room again but before he could take a step, something hit him over the head. Everything went dark.

12

Madison took an Ambien before bed. Anything to help her sleep.

She had a dream about her dad that felt so real. They were sitting together in the family room of her childhood home. Dad was wearing his favorite bathrobe and slippers that he always wore around the house. They were chatting as if he was still alive.

"Dad, I love you and miss you so much."

"Madison, I love you too. I can hear you when you talk to me. I'm sorry I'm not always able to show I'm listening. Just know I'll always be here with you."

Madison gave her dad a big embrace. She didn't want to ever let go of him. Slowly, her surroundings became hazy. Dad and the living room disappeared. Madison awoke.

She tried to shut her eyes again hopeful she could escape back to her dreams, but she was unsuccessful. Tears streamed down her face as reality set in. She then heard beeping. Her phone's alarm. It was 5 a.m.

They hadn't stayed out too late last night, though Jessica had wanted to. But what was bothering Bradley? The text was more than strange. He'd never done that before. *I hate you.* Maybe it was a joke? She'd asked where he was and what was wrong, but she had yet to hear back from him.

The sunrise hike at Cowles Mountain was glorious and calming, the highest point in San Diego. Hopefully, it wouldn't be too crowded this morning. Through the window, the early morning sky was dark and foggy. Should be okay.

She jumped out of bed and put on Lululemon shorts, a T-shirt, and hat. She brushed her teeth, packed an apple, filled a water bottle, fed Penelope, and headed out the door, anxious to catch the sunrise.

It usually took less than an hour. One-and-a-half-miles to breathtaking views of the desert mountains to the east, the ocean to the west, and on a clear day, the city skyline. The trailhead was fifteen minutes from the apartment. It would be close.

A few other cars sat in the dark lot but it wasn't as busy as usual. She looked up at the dusky sky and mountain summit covered in thick clouds. Might not be the best day to hike. The fog will surely cover the sunrise. But at least it will be a good workout.

She used the flashlight on her phone to guide her way to the top, though, she could have done it in the dark, familiar as she was with every root and rock. She passed a few hikers on the way but otherwise, the mountain was eerily quiet. Too quiet, perhaps. And a chill settled into her spine and made its way up to her neck.

She could take quiet, a momentary lapse in conversation, a break in the noise, but complete and elongated silence was no good. She stopped and removed the pack from her shoulders, settled it on her thigh, and fished for the small case in the zipper pocket. A crack of a branch sounded somewhere to the left and she resisted the urge to jump. It's just a squirrel, Madison. Or a coyote. Get it together, girl. Amy's face floated before her in the dusk and she shook it away. Not now.

With EarPods secured, she scrolled through her playlists and chose 'Survivor' by Destiny's Child, took a few deep breaths, pumped her arms and legs a few times then shook the tension out before continuing the ascent. After forty-five minutes of rocky terrain and patches of low-lying brush, she reached the summit.

The sky was starting to brighten through the thick blanket of fog. It was 6:15 a.m. No way she would see the sunrise in this.

A steady wind picked up as she cleared the patch of fog, and for a moment, it seemed hopeful the sun might appear, but then another patch moved in. Visibility was shifty. One moment, she could make out the eastern horizon, the next she could barely see five feet in front of her.

She removed the EarPods and reached for her phone to check her messages. Bradley was still MIA. Very unlike him. He was usually responsive. She texted Jessica.

Hey—you hear anything from Bradley? That was a weird text we received from him last night. Hopefully he got home safe.

The text barely went through—signal was spotty at the top of the mountain.

After resting for a few moments, she began her descent, passing a few hikers. Visibility still bad, she moved more slowly than usual and after about fifteen minutes, stopped to catch her breath.

A loud crunch sounded in the distance, off the trail. Bigger than a coyote. She turned around. Must be a hiker taking a piss out of sight. The fog was getting thicker. Three-foot visibility. She stepped a few feet up the trail. No one. Another crunch sounded behind her, this time much closer than before.

"Hello, is anybody there?"

Suddenly, a jogger ran into her, nearly knocking her to the ground. "Sorry," he said and darted off into the distance.

"You almost took me down, you know! Watch where you're going!" She yelled out as she stumbled to the side.

By then, the man was already well ahead of her. A waste of time yelling. He was wearing headphones.

Perplexing how people were able to run down the mountain, even on a perfectly clear day, the path filled with jagged rocks and occasional boulders. An easy way to break a leg or sprain an ankle, at least. Accidents happened on the mountain all the time.

She took a few steps down the trail and listened but it was quiet again. Still, she felt strange, like someone was following close behind her. Every few steps, she stopped and listened but nothing. It wasn't another hiker. It was the same feeling she had in Grand Central Station last month.

She picked up her pace, anxious to get to the bottom of the mountain and to her car. She occasionally glanced over her shoulder, expecting to see someone, but no one. A looming dread worsened with each step.

Her phone vibrated in her pack and she reached for the zipper on the front pouch, not stopping. She pulled out the phone. A missed call and a new text message from Jessica.

You are not going to believe this. Bradley is in the hospital! He was apparently knocked unconscious and found bleeding in the dance studio last night.

One of the dance instructors, Lexi, forgot her purse and found him.

She texted me early this morning. I'm trying to find out what hospital he is in so as soon as I have more info I will let you know!

This was all too much. Amy, Kristin, Jared, and now Bradley? Madison needed to get to the car.

A brisk walk turned into a run. She jumped a root system and nearly stumbled before cornering a boulder, her right foot sliding a little too far out to the side. She landed on her knee. Footsteps definitely behind her now. They weren't slowing. She looked around her and into the fog. There was no one there. She crouched down, the boulder to her back, as a new patch of fog rolled around her, obscuring visibility completely. She listened for footsteps.

The fog dissipated a little. Still, no one there. The phone vibrated. Jessica.

Okay, so Bradley is at Scripps Hospital. I'm headed there in a few. Apparently, he is conscious and doing okay. He's giving a report to authorities now.

Madison's hands were trembling. She pulled them to her mouth and breathed on them, trying to warm them, but they were ice cold. No doubt about it now. Amy's killer attacked Bradley.

Finally, the fog cleared. She stood and started down the mountain again, making it around the next bend, when a crack sounded behind her. She turned. The fog had cleared completely. On the trail, above her, stood a figure who must have been the killer in a dark, faceless mask, holding a hunting knife in the air and turning the blade, showing it to her. It was black as night. Brown leather handle.

"No." She backed away and, with each step the killer, lean and muscular, took a step forward with a boxy sort of swagger. Definitely male. She set her jaw and braced her muscles, ready to leap away. She anchored her feet and stared straight into the faceless mask with every fiber.

"I said no." It was low and firm.

The killer started and she spun, sprinting down the mountain, long, striding leaps over roots, vaulting boulders. He might catch her but it wouldn't be without a fight. She glanced back from time to time. He had gained a little but she knew the trail. She was light and nimble. At one point he stumbled and fell flat on his stomach. He lay there a moment and pounded the dirt. It was an odd gesture, something a child would do. She watched him from a distance, dialing 9-1-1 but the one bar she had was now gone.

He pulled himself up and she turned, running again, heart pounding, legs numb now. The adrenaline focused her but she couldn't keep going like this the entire descent.

The wooden footbridge was just ahead, a quarter mile from the base. She had him by at least one bend, now. If she could obstruct his path, somehow. She jumped onto the footbridge and her left foot caught the front, twisting her ankle as she fell. A sharp pain jutted through her leg. "Shit!" No way to outrun him now. She looked left and right then heard a soft rush of movement below. It wasn't the best hiding place but it would have to do.

She pushed her body off the side of the bridge and fell three feet down into the ravine. There wasn't much to cover her, so she grabbed handfuls of dirt and rubbed it onto her arms, legs, face, over her T-shirt and shorts, anything to camouflage her. A bird suddenly flew into the ravine, landing in front of a small crawl space beneath the bridge. She hadn't seen it as it was covered by brush. Madison belly-crawled and squeezed inside.

It was seconds before she heard the footsteps. Between the cracks in the footbridge, she saw the black soles of the boots above her. She covered her mouth and nose, not daring to breathe, and jumped a little when the knife glinted through the cracks. He was almost across the bridge entirely when he suddenly stopped and looked side to side.

He must know I'm watching him. He can feel my eyes on him the same way I felt his.

She pulled out her phone, no signal, and put it on silent. He would hear the vibration.

He paced a few more seconds, crossing the footbridge then disappearing into the fog. She lay in the crawl space for what seemed an hour, listening for his footsteps. Finally, she crawled out and onto the bridge. No signal, still.

The bird returned, as if to comfort her. She took off her left shoe to assess the damage. Minor swelling. Didn't look too bad. A group of hikers approached in the distance. The bird flew away. She tried to brush some of the dirt from her arms and legs.

One of the hikers, a middle-aged man, called out to help her. "Ma'am, are you okay? Did you fall off the bridge? Can we help you get up at all?"

"I was chased. A man with a knife. He had a mask. I hid under the bridge till he left."

All of them looked into the trees. The man said, "Are you sure he is gone? Let's get you out of here. Did you call 9-1-1?" He gestured to her phone.

"No service."

"Let's go." Two of the younger hikers, a man and a woman, walked by her side, holding her up, as they made their way down the mountain. When they were in the parking lot and beside their cars, everyone calmed a little. The older man tried to call 9-1-1.

The woman offered her a water bottle. "No thank you. I have some. Did you see anyone suspicious on your way up?"

"No," the woman said. "We didn't see anyone. It's been quieter than normal here today because of the fog. Did he hurt you?"

"No. My ankle just hurts a little." She turned to the older man. "Any service?"

"Not yet. Check your phone now."

Madison looked. Two bars.

"I do. Calling 9-1-1." She put her phone on speaker so the hikers could hear.

A woman on the other end picked up.

"9-1-1...what's your emergency?"

"Hello—yes...I was just chased by a masked assailant at Cowles Mountain. He was carrying a knife."

"Are you still being chased? Are you in a safe place?"

"Yes—I'm safe now. He ran off. Three other hikers helped bring me down the mountain."

"I'll send police there right now."

Madison remembered Bradley was in the hospital. And Jessica mentioned he was giving a report to the police.

"Actually—I think my friend was attacked last night by the same person in Mission Beach. He's at Scripps Hospital now being interviewed by authorities. I can give a statement there."

The woman responded, "Are you okay to drive?"

The hikers looked at each other and whispered to Madison, "We'll drive you."

Madison focused her attention back on her conversation with the operator.

"The hikers who found me have offered to drive. I should be there in twenty minutes."

"Okay, ma'am. I'll contact dispatch to let them know you are on the way. Please call us back if you see the attacker again."

Madison was guided to the female hiker's car and she climbed in the backseat.

She immediately texted Jessica.

Hey, Jess, in a complete daze right now. During my hike, I was chased by the killer. Definitely male. He had a knife. I was able to get away and am safe now.

Jessica responded.

Oh my gosh, you weren't hurt, were you? I'm driving to Scripps right now. There may be cops there you can speak to.

Madison continued to feverously type.

I'm okay. Thankfully wasn't stabbed. Just a sore ankle. I called 9-1-1 and told them I'm on the way to the hospital to give a report. I will see you in twenty minutes.

Madison looked out the window and realized the car was already speeding down the freeway.

13

Two uniformed officers, a man and a woman, stood in the hallway outside Bradley's room.

Inside, Jessica sat in a chair by Bradley's bed, both of them gazing up at the beautiful Doctor Hernandez. Bradley flashed his patented smile, explaining that his parents were flying from Michigan and would be there by nightfall. He didn't need to stay overnight, but the doctor wouldn't have it.

"A precaution." Doctor Hernandez smiled and Jessica giggled a little. Bradley gave her a glare, which meant back off. Doctor Hernandez was his.

The MRI showed no bruising or bleeding in the brain. He likely suffered a mild concussion. "I'll give you a script for the pain," Doctor Hernandez said.

"If you think that's best," Bradley said and smiled again.

Doctor Hernandez left for his rounds and the two officers entered. The female officer turned to Madison. "Are you the one that was chased this morning on Cowles Mountain?"

"Yes, ma'am."

The officers led Madison to a vacant room. She started at the beginning, discussing the on-going murder investigation for Amy, Kristin, and Jared. No official suspects had been named. This all led up to Bradley being attacked at the dance studio and her being chased by the killer earlier that morning.

"What was this individual wearing?"

"He was wearing all black and a gray mask. It was faceless. No mouth, and the eyes were covered with something. He could see out but I couldn't see in. He had what looked like a hunting knife. It had a black blade and brown leather handle."

"How do you know it was a he?"

"The way he moved. The body structure."

"Sounds like your friend's attacker. Did he say anything? Was the voice recognizable?"

"He said nothing."

"What else can you tell us? Height?"

"About average for a guy. Taller than me."

"Do you have any people in your life that would have reason to do something like this to you and those close to you?"

"No one I can think of."

"Any ex-boyfriends? Jealousy can make people do bad things."

"I broke up with my boyfriend Kyle recently, but we ended things amicably. He's never shown any tendencies toward violence. He couldn't do something like this."

"Give us his last name. We're not saying he's involved but we'll need to check in with him."

"Sorrento. He actually works at this hospital."

She answered the rest of their questions and they did the friendly community officer thing. They advised her to be alert and stay with Jessica or Bradley for the time being. Call the department if she thinks of anything more or if there are any additional incidents.

Madison exited the room and found Jessica sitting in a chair outside Bradley's hospital room, looking down at her phone. "How did it go?"

"Fine. I told them everything that's happened over the past several weeks. They told me to stay in contact if anything further happens. Same thing. But they don't know who it is."

"Do *you* have any clue who it is? After today?"

"I think it's a man. Other than that, I couldn't tell. He wore all black, head to foot. The mask covered everything. No mouth. The eyes had these filters. I couldn't see in. Didn't get close enough to see in, to be honest. I ran like hell."

"Yes, you did. Because you, chica, are a bad ass bitch."

They laughed a little as a familiar face turned the corner and walked down the hall. Black hair, green eyes, handsome face, and tanned skin. He was in nurse scrubs.

Jessica turned to see what Madison was staring at. "Oh," she said and stood. "I'll leave you two alone." She walked into Bradley's room as Kyle stepped in front of Madison.

"Hi," he said with a start. He stepped closer to Madison and stopped, surprised to see her. "Everything okay?"

She was suddenly aware of the state of her clothes and body, covered in dirt. She felt awkward now that she knew her dad said no when Kyle asked for her hand in marriage last year.

"Hi, Kyle. I'm okay. It's been a crazy morning."

"Is there anything I can do?"

"Bradley was attacked last night." She gestured to the hospital room as her eyes started to swell. "I was chased this morning. Three people close to me have been murdered."

"Oh my God. I'm so sorry. I knew about Amy. Who else?"

"Kristin and Jared. I worked with them, remember?"

"I would like to help but want to give you space. Respect your privacy. I know we aren't together, anymore, but I still care."

She wobbled a little on her feet and Kyle put a hand on her arm.

"Thank you. I appreciate it. I'm just tired. I really don't want to hold you up—I'll let you get back to work."

"I need to go pick up some prescriptions for my patients. Why don't you come with me? It will give us a chance to catch up."

She hesitated but figured it wouldn't hurt. She walked with Kyle down the hall as he led her into a room with a giant machine.

"What's that for?"

"It's an automated dispensing medicine cabinet. Essentially a computerized medicine cabinet for hospitals. Stores all the medications I need for my patients."

Today was the first day Madison saw Kyle on the job as a nurse. The most she had done before now was drop him off and pick him up when his truck was in the repair shop. She'd never been inside. She hated hospitals. He placed his finger up to the machine.

"Takes fingerprints to control access." He continued making selections on the computer screen. "How's your mom doing by the way? Know it's been hard for her since your dad passed."

"I stayed with her when I went back for Amy's funeral. It was good to see her. She's lonely. Still trying to process everything that's happened." A drawer underneath Kyle suddenly opened. He reached down and pressed another button, which opened a box that held several prescriptions. He grabbed one of the vials. He held it up so she could see.

"Insulin. For one of my patients with diabetes."

Madison nodded her head. Kyle then reached into a container above him and pulled out a syringe. It reminded her of something.

The mysterious needle prick on Dad's arm the day he died.

Kyle had access to any prescription he desired as a nurse. She looked at the vial of insulin in his hand. She remembered from one of her college biology classes that insulin poisoning could be fatal. Had they tested for insulin on Dad's toxicology test?

Kyle waved a hand in her face. "Madison, you okay? You look uneasy."

Don't give yourself away, Madison. Act normal.

"Yeah, I'm fine. I think just being in a hospital is difficult. Brings back memories of Dad."

"Well, let's get out of here then. I'll bring you back to Bradley's hospital room and, hopefully, you can head out soon."

They turned and walked down the hallway toward Bradley. Once outside, Kyle gave her a tepid hug.

"Don't be a stranger."

He ran into his co-worker Aaron, who smiled at Madison, and then Kyle walked the other way, still carrying the vial of insulin and syringe. After she could no longer see him, the tears came.

Could Kyle be the killer?

14

A killer was on the loose and she was now a target. Her ex-boyfriend could be responsible for the murders of not just Amy, Jared, and Kristin, but Dad as well. After saying goodbye to Bradley, she stepped into the hospital hallway and leaned up against the wall. She pulled out her phone. A new text message from Zane.

Hey, Mom's really worried about you. How about we meet halfway in Dana Point for dinner tonight? I don't mind driving down. It will be good for you to get out of San Diego anyways.

She would respond later.

First, she Googled insulin poisoning. Countless articles appeared. One called it the perfect murder. There was a case that involved a wife who murdered her husband by injecting lethal doses of insulin into him. She was a nurse. *Killer nurse.*

Madison pulled up her emails. She looked for Dad's toxicology results from January. She opened the email with the attachment. Negative test results for everything—amphetamines, barbiturates, methamphetamine, opiates. She didn't see hormones listed, which insulin would fall under. On the sheet was the phone number for the testing lab. She dialed immediately. A woman on the other end answered.

"Hello, how can I help you?"

"Hello, I would like to inquire about some test results." She whispered and looked around. No sign of Kyle. She didn't want him to hear.

"Sure. Please give me the report number."

Madison gave the woman the number and heard her type. "Okay, I have the report pulled up on my screen."

"Was this specimen tested for insulin?"

"We don't test for insulin poisoning, ma'am. It's not routinely offered by most forensic toxicology laboratories. It's very challenging and complex to test for."

"Thanks."

Madison hung up the phone. It was certain something unsuspecting and common like insulin would have gone undetected in Dad's toxicology test. Kyle would have both the knowledge and the access to it as an ER nurse. She was also not with him when Dad went into cardiac arrest. She assumed he was out buying flowers, but he could have been anywhere.

Where was Kyle on the night of Amy's murder? Work would be a possibility. Someone at Scripps Hospital should be able to pull up his attendance record, but she couldn't ask just anyone. It had to be someone that already knew her. Suddenly, she saw Aaron turn the corner ahead. Kyle was no longer with him. Kyle had once told her he thought Aaron had a crush on her. She ran down the hall to catch up with him. He was logging into a portable computer station in the hall.

"Aaron, can you look something up for me quickly?"

"Hey. I'm pretty busy with a patient right now. What is it?"

She had to think of a viable story. *Think, Madison. Think.*

"Well, you know how Kyle and I broke up, right? I always suspected he was cheating on me."

Hopefully Kyle hadn't disclosed details of their break-up to Aaron. He seemed to be buying her story so far. She continued.

"Well, he told me he was working April 1st and 2nd, but I secretly always thought he was meeting up with another girl. Can you check his work attendance record for me on those days?"

"I'm really busy. I—"

"Please, Aaron." She reached for his arm and caressed it gently. "For closure."

He shrugged. "Fine. Can't say no to a pretty girl like you." He began typing on the computer and pulled up their employee calendar, with schedule and time tracking. She saw April 1st and 2nd were grayed out.

"What does that mean?"

He responded, "Well looks like he called in sick both of those days. He was here on April 3rd though."

She knew what this meant. Kyle had every opportunity to fly back east, kill Amy, and then take an early morning direct flight back to San Diego. With the time change, he would have gotten back just in time to pick up the last of his belongings from Madison's apartment later that day.

"Thanks, Aaron! One more thing. Are you able to look up transactions on that automated medicine machine?"

"Yeah—we are able to pull up those records."

"Well, I've suspected Kyle may be stealing medication, specifically insulin. Can you look up his transaction history for me?"

"That's a big accusation. As much as I want to help you, I really have to get back to my patient."

"How about if I give you my number and you can get back to me?" If Aaron had a crush on her, surely he wouldn't mind taking her number. He smiled and pulled out his phone as she provided it to him. She was still caressing his arm.

"Thanks. Please let me know what you find out." She lifted her hand off his arm and ran down the hallway toward the exit. She remembered Zane's text and responded.

Hey, let's meet up. A lot has happened today. My friend Bradley is in the hospital after being attacked. I was chased by the killer. Let's plan for an early dinner at 5 p.m. at Dana Point Harbor.

First, she had to take an Uber back to Cowles Mountain to pick up her car. Luckily she also had a change of clothes in her gym bag that was in there. After being dropped off at her car and driving for over an hour, she arrived in Dana Point shortly before 5 p.m. It was a cool day—May Gray had blanketed the coast with thick clouds. On the drive up, there was even fog and drizzle. Once seated at the restaurant outside along the harbor, peaks of sunshine started to filter through the clouds.

Madison ordered a martini as she waited for her brother to arrive. Just as the waitress brought over her beverage, she spotted Zane approach the table. He was in a camouflage hoodie and blue jeans.

"Hey, sorry I'm a little late. Traffic getting out of LA was bad, as usual."

He quickly wrapped his arms around her and held her tight for several seconds. She didn't want to let go. She needed her big brother.

"No worries at all. Thanks so much for being here. Really needed to see you. I already ordered a drink."

The waitress stopped by and Zane ordered a whiskey on the rocks. Madison took another sip of her martini.

"You were attacked? What happened? Tell me everything. And your friend Bradley too?"

"Yeah, I was chased but never physically hurt. Just a sore ankle. Thankfully Bradley is okay. He should be released from the hospital soon."

"I assume you're in contact with the police?"

"Yes, I spoke with the police again at the hospital today. No update regarding possible suspects."

"Am I officially off your list?"

"Zane, not funny. Anyway, something clicked for me earlier when I was at the hospital and ran into Kyle. Have you ever heard of insulin poisoning before?"

"I mean, I don't think so, but I guess it could happen. Too much of anything is never good, right?"

"What happens if Kyle injected Dad with enough insulin to kill him? And then went after me and my friends? Angry at Dad for not giving permission to marry me. I think Kyle sensed around the time of Dad's death that I wanted to break-up with him. Jealous ex-boyfriend out for revenge."

"Well, anything is possible. But didn't they do a toxicology test on Dad and it came back negative?"

"Yes, but I called the testing lab and they don't test for insulin poisoning."

"Do you still really think it was something else that killed him other than the attack? He was already so weak from the cancer…"

Madison interjected, "I've always been suspicious."

Zane continued, "Well, it seems like a crazy theory but it's possible. What are you going to do about it?"

"See if I can get a record of Kyle's medication transactions from the hospital."

"Just be vigilant. Don't put yourself in any danger. I worry about you staying all alone in your place."

"Honestly I feel my apartment is pretty safe with all the building security."

"You should go back and stay with Mom for a little while. Get out of town. There's also the family vacation house on Cape Cod. You could stay there with some friends and lay low."

Madison looked down at her phone to check the date. Zane had a good point. It was only a few weeks away from Memorial Day weekend—maybe a getaway with some of her friends wouldn't be such a bad idea. Life had been so unforgiving these past few months that she desperately needed to get away. It could also be a good opportunity to reconnect with Dawn, whose family also had a house on the Cape.

"Not a bad idea. Definitely going to think about it. Why don't you come with? I'd love to spend some more quality time with you."

"Work is consuming so much of my time. Recently got promoted to sales manager. That's why I've been going to our New York office a lot lately. Otherwise, I would."

She was still annoyed he hadn't told her the details of being fired from Dad's company, but for now, it seemed like Zane was turning over a new leaf. His past transgressions were hopefully behind him.

"That's good, Zane. I bet Mom's proud of you too. I'm glad you have been keeping in touch with her. I know she appreciates it when you call her."

"Yeah, just wish I had time to see her more. She spoke to you about Dad's will, right?"

"She did mention it when I was home last month."

After finishing dinner and walking along the harbor, she hugged Zane goodbye in the parking lot.

"Don't be a stranger, sis. Call me anytime. If I'm not traveling, I'm close and can be in San Diego in two hours."

"Thanks. I'll text you when I get home."

Once in her car, she sat there with her hand on the steering wheel and took a deep breath. What a day. She needed an escape. She remembered Zane mentioning the Cape. Not a bad idea. She reached for her phone in her purse to text Dawn.

Hey—what are you up to Memorial Day weekend? Thinking of getting out of California for a bit and heading to the Cape. You have anything planned?

She waited for a few minutes before noticing that Dawn was already texting a response.

Funny you should ask. I'm having a Memorial Day party at my parent's house on the Cape. Perfect way to welcome the unofficial start of summer. Parents will be on a three-week cruise around the Mediterranean. You should totally come! Bring whoever.

Madison then texted Jessica.

Hey Jess—how do you feel about coming with me to the Cape for Memorial Day weekend? I need to get out of California.

Jessica responded a few minutes later.

Chica, you think they will let you leave the state with the on-going investigation? Are you going to invite Bradley?

Madison responded.

I mean it's not like I'm a suspect. Plus if I say it's to see family, I don't see why they wouldn't allow it. I'll ask Bradley in a few days. Too soon right now.

Jessica sent another text.

Count me in then. By the way, was just invited by my friend Raquel who is a fashion editor at Vogue to the Louis Vuitton Fashion Show on Thursday at Salk Institute. Used to dance with her in high school. Looks like a cool event but not sure if I'm in the mood to go. Feel bad with everything that's happened. I'd be up for watching movies at your apartment and keeping you company instead if you like?

Madison responded.

Go! I appreciate the concern but that's supposed to be an amazing event. That venue in La Jolla is stunning. Don't miss it. I'll be fine. Have fun and be safe!

LA JOLLA, CALIFORNIA

Thursday, May 12, 2022
7 p.m.

Concrete, glass, and steel—austere materials. But enduring. The gray concrete slab Jessica sat on was cold to the touch. Two mirror-image concrete buildings rose above the central courtyard. A thin, linear water stream cut through the concrete floor of the courtyard and flowed toward the Pacific Ocean in the background.

The setting sun made the water in the stream and ocean glisten.

"Raquel, is that Emma Roberts sitting over there?"

Jessica pointed to the row of concrete slabs across from them.

"Sure is, Jess."

"Oh my gosh, I love her! Especially in *Scream Queens*! She was a genius in that show! Such a bad ass chica!"

"Oh, and look over there. Two sections down from Emma. Leslie Mann!"

"I cannot! At this rate, I'll be staring at the attendees more than the models."

"I wouldn't say that yet. The show hasn't even started."

Jessica by now had forgotten she was sitting on the most uncomfortable seat possible.

As the sun dipped closer to the horizon, the models began to traverse the concrete runway. The glamorous '80s-inspired synth hook of The Weeknd's 'Blinding Lights' erupted over the sound system. It looked like a setting out of the movie *Dune*—futuristic bolero and bomber jackets, metallic pants, space-age shoulder pads, and jacquard gowns. The whole setting looked post-apocalyptic.

"These women look like superheroine goddesses," Jessica whispered to Raquel.

Some carried skateboards. Others sported metallic striped boots, chains, and sneakers. Many mirrored the modern architecture of the Salk Institute, while some of the billowing and flowing silhouettes mimicked the ocean waves.

"This is Louis Vuitton's 2023 collection," Raquel responded.

Jessica felt like she was in a movie. A nice escape from reality. She hoped Madison and Bradley were okay. She wished they could be here to enjoy this moment with her. Should she feel guilty for being here with everything that had happened?

Halfway through the show, Jessica whispered to her friend, "Need to use the ladies' room. I'll be back soon."

"Okay, hurry up. Don't want you to miss the end!"

Jessica looked behind her and spotted the entrance to one of the concrete buildings that rose above her. She stood up, trying her best to duck down so as not to obstruct the view of people sitting behind her. She slid past and briskly walked toward the door.

With one tug of the handle, she was relieved to find that it was unlocked. She entered the building and marveled at the unadorned interior with high, cathedral-like ceilings. She spotted a sign for the bathroom past the foyer down the hall. As she walked, she noticed portraits lined the walls. Researchers in molecular biology, genetics, and neuroscience. This was a world-renowned research institute after all—a cathedral to science.

But also a cathedral to art—architecture, and now fashion. Science and art, drawing from the same creative source.

The building was empty. There wasn't a person in sight as she finally reached the bathroom door. No one wanted to miss the show.

Once inside the restroom, Jessica walked up to the mirror. After placing her purse on the sink, she pulled out her Xanax prescription. It worked wonders for the social anxiety she secretly battled with—no one would ever guess based on her usual vibrant and bubbly personality. She needed to take the edge off tonight. She placed one pill in her mouth and swallowed it before looking back at her reflection once more.

I need to text Madison and Bradley.

She reached for her phone. Hopefully they weren't mad at her for attending such a lavish event. Madison had encouraged her to go. She would have spoken up if she had an issue with it.

Hola amores—just wanted to check in to see how you both are doing. Fashion show is fun. But I miss you guys.

After she hit send, the lights in the bathroom turned off. Jessica stood there in complete darkness.

"Hello, is anybody there?" she called out.

She heard the slow drip of a faucet near her. It reverberated against the concrete walls.

Her eyes eventually adjusted to the darkness, and the dim red glow of the exit sign on the doorway provided some light. Before she could find the light switch, she heard a sound come from one of the three stalls. She turned around and could faintly see that all three doors were closed. She walked forward and raised her hand to open the first one.

No one was inside.

She stepped to the left and opened the second.

Empty.

Finally, she reached the third door. Before opening it, she paused and took a deep breath. With her hand trembling slightly, she raised her hand and opened the third door. It swung open and hit the wall inside.

Also empty.

Jessica breathed a sigh of relief, unsure why she was so scared in the first place. The Xanax had yet to kick-in.

She turned her body back around toward the mirrors but instead of her reflection, a figure stood in front of her. They were dressed in all black and wearing a gray faceless mask, the same color as the concrete walls. Black eyes stared back at her.

Before she could scream, the figure put its hand over her mouth and pushed her into one of the stalls. She kicked and punched but was completely taken by surprise and overpowered quickly. The stall door slammed shut and was now locked.

As a struggle ensued in the stall, she saw light and heard the door to the main entrance of the bathroom swing open. One of the fashion show attendees? She desperately tried to scream, but the assailant was still holding their hand over her mouth. All that came out was a series of moans.

She heard a woman's voice yell, "Eww…get a room!"

The bathroom door slammed shut.

The masked figure removed their left hand from Jessica's mouth and choked her aggressively. She kicked and tried to free herself, but the grip was too tight and she had to try to gasp for breath. She swung her fist to attempt to free herself but was unsuccessful. The pain and lack of oxygen made her hazy. With each move, she felt she was gradually losing consciousness.

In the chaos of the moment, she saw a black knife blade in the individual's right hand.

I'm not going to die tonight.

The attacker had to be male. Tall. Broad shoulders. Moved like a man.

Go for the groin, Jessica.

Adrenaline suddenly surged through her body. She lifted her knee and swung it as hard as she could in the groin.

A sudden moan. They winced and loosened their grip around her neck.

She found the latch to the stall door, unlocked it, and staggered out as she gasped for breath. She saw the glow of the exit sign and was able to make it to the bathroom door.

Once outside, she ran down the empty concrete hallway toward the central courtyard screaming for help. Each scream vibrated. Minimalism overtaken by chaos.

Just like the concrete, glass, and steel that surrounded her, Jessica was determined to survive.

15

Madison received a call from Jessica early Friday morning about the attack. Her heart sank when she called crying. She couldn't recall ever hearing Jessica this upset.

They agreed to meet up, along with Bradley, that Sunday evening on Coronado Beach to watch the sunset. A time to reflect and be thankful they were still alive. All three friends as survivors. Madison took off her sandals and felt the soft, white sand between her toes. It was fine and gentle to the touch. White, puffy clouds dotted the skyline. It would be a stunning sunset tonight.

Madison set a blanket down, large enough for the three of them, several feet from the shoreline. Right on top of the last strip of dry sand before it turned wet. Jessica proceeded down to the water's edge and dipped her toes in.

"How cold is it?" Madison yelled.

"Cold as ice," Jessica responded.

She walked back to the blanket and sat in the middle.

"Just being here makes me appreciate the beauty of the things we take for granted. Madison, thanks for convincing me to come out. Been holed up in my apartment the past couple of days after getting checked at the hospital."

"I don't blame you. Just thankful you were able to get away. How's your neck?"

Jessica pulled down her hoodie. Madison saw the purple marks—they still looked fresh.

"It was worse on Friday. Thankfully no internal damage or anything. Just some bad bruising."

"Well, looks like we all suffered some battle wounds from our encounter. We are a couple of bad ass friends. If anything, we've proved that no one should try and fuck with us." Madison and Jessica laughed. Bradley pulled aside the hair on the right side of his head to show stitches.

"Jess, what did you end up telling authorities?" Madison reached her arm around her friend to embrace her as all three friends sat and looked toward the ocean.

"Everything. How I was choked, nearly strangled to death—almost stabbed too. Told them what the attacker looked like. Gray faceless mask. Black eyes. I couldn't even see through enough to tell what the person's eye color was. Black knife blade. Looked like a leather handle. Hunting knife maybe? Exactly how you guys described it. And it had to be a guy. The way he moved. Kicked him in his groin too and that caused pain."

"Thank God you got away. Things could have turned out so much worse. For all three of us."

Bradley nodded his head in agreement.

"Who could be doing this? Honestly. I'm at a loss for words. We're all being targeted, and I don't see an end in sight." Jessica appeared frustrated, a far cry from her usual jubilant personality.

Madison hadn't yet told her friends about her suspicion of Kyle. She received a text back last night from Aaron, Kyle's nurse co-worker, about the medication withdrawals which didn't reveal the smoking gun she had hoped for.

Hey—don't think Kyle's been stealing medication. All of his transactions on the system are tied to a medication order. No overrides. Didn't see any large withdrawal of insulin. By the way, you up to grab a drink this weekend?

"No clue. I've thought through it so much, and I'm still where I was a week ago. Maybe even more confused." Madison removed her arm from Jessica's shoulder, folded her arms, and put her head down.

Bradley responded, "Maybe we were targeted at random. None of us can think of anyone in our lives that would want to do this, right? Maybe this is a case of some random nutjob serial killer."

"Anything is possible, I guess. I've just never heard of a serial killer that's targeted one specific group of friends and not known them. This isn't *Friday the 13th* where we are all counselors at some sleep away camp in the woods," Jessica responded.

The sun inched closer to the horizon.

"By the way, are you still going to the Cape next weekend for Memorial Day?"

"Yes, still planning on it. I ran it by my mom and she's letting me have the vacation house for the long weekend. Said I could bring some friends too."

Jessica interjected, "Good, because I need to get the hell out of here. That's if I'm still invited."

"Of course you are. I need you there. When you spoke to the

authorities, did you mention anything about leaving town?"

"I did. Originally, they didn't want me to go. Any of us for that matter, since we are all tied in with the investigation now. I asked them straight up if any of us were suspects. They said no. I mean we were all attacked. We were together the night your friend Amy was murdered. So there's nothing they can do to prevent us from going. Plus, I told them it would probably be safer to leave for a little while. Hopefully throw the killer off track. Maybe this will all just go away…"

Bradley looked at Jessica. "As much as I want this to go away too, we have to find out who is doing this. I don't want to live in fear all my life."

"Are you coming with us by the way, Bradley?" Madison inquired.

"Even if I lost a limb, I'd probably find a way to come. Not going to let a little concussion stop me. This killer is going to have to try harder than that."

"Well, it's good to know we will be together next week. I feel good knowing we have each other's backs," Madison reasoned. "We will make it through this alive."

The sun dipped below the horizon. The white puffy clouds turned an ominous red. Blood red. They reflected against the ocean. Madison felt as though she was in a snow globe. But instead of snow, she was surrounded by a sea of blood. The waves began to pick up in intensity, crashing against the shore. A seagull flew along the surface of the water, gliding effortlessly. Madison placed her hands in the hoodie she was wearing and followed the seagull with her eyes as it flew. She briefly closed her eyes.

She remembered when she first moved to San Diego—her and Dad had visited Coronado Beach for sunset that first weekend. It was a cool evening, with even more clouds than tonight. They'd sat on the sand, forgetting to bring a blanket. Madison had brought her portable speaker. They were listening to 'Another Day in Paradise' by Phil Collins. One of Dad's favorites.

As the sun was setting, they saw a seal jump from the water. Then another. And a third. The three continued to take turns to jump. She remembered the conversation with Dad.

"You know what seals represent, don't you Madison?"

Madison shrugged her shoulders.

"No clue, Dad. I do know they are adorable."

"They are adorable. They are also highly imaginative and playful creatures. Almost like children in a way. A seal is supposed to inspire creativity in your life. Notice how those seals are playing with each other. They are symbols for awakening your inner child to bring joy to your life. They are explorers and need to constantly challenge their minds to find interesting things around them. They are always on the move."

"I could probably take a lesson from them then," Madison joked.

"Don't ever settle, Madison. Think back to what excited you as a kid. Don't let that dream die."

Madison opened her eyes and was back on the beach with her friends. The seagull was gone. The clouds had now turned a softer shade of red. Almost pink.

"You okay?" Bradley gently touched Madison's shoulder.

Hopefully he didn't see the tears that were starting to form. She brushed them away. She didn't want to make this moment about her sense of loss—not only her friends, but her Dad.

"I'm fine. Just got sand in my eye."

"It's okay to be vulnerable." Jessica now returned the favor and put her arm around her. "Like you said, we will get through this together."

Though Madison wanted to believe Jessica's reassuring words, deep down she worried that at least one of them would not make it out alive.

16

Memorial Day weekend had finally arrived. Madison and her friends needed a break from their new reality. They were leaving California with no additional information on who killed Amy, Jared, and Kristin, nor who attacked them. Authorities tried to persuade them to stay in support of the on-going investigation but ultimately did not prohibit them from traveling. The group reiterated they felt safer leaving.

A few local news outlets wanted to interview them, but each of them declined. Better to get away and avoid any publicity. Madison, Bradley, and Jessica were on strict orders not to post on social media while they were traveling, just in case it tipped off the killer as to their location.

Since Madison had grown up spending summers on Cape Cod, she hoped she would be a good tour guide for her friends—though she wished they were going on happier terms. There was no better place to kick-start an early summer and experience quintessential New England.

They departed San Diego on a red-eye flight and arrived in Boston early on Saturday morning. After grabbing their checked baggage, they took the shuttle to pick up their rental car—a Jeep Wrangler, the perfect vehicle for exploring the Cape. After packing their luggage into the Jeep, they briefly met up with Madison's mom who was in Boston for the day. Madison had brought her dog, Penelope, on the flight, and her mother offered to take care of her as Madison and her friends enjoyed the Cape house.

"Thanks, Mom for watching Penelope for me. And, for letting us enjoy the house for the long weekend."

"Of course. You guys just be safe. Here are the keys to the house. Are you sure you don't want me to stay there with you?"

She handed the keychain over.

"No. We'll be okay."

"Well, Connecticut is only a three-hour drive away. I can be there quick. Don't hesitate to call me if you need anything."

"I won't."

"Tell Dawn I say 'Hi' by the way. Glad you will get a chance to reconnect with her."

"Yeah, she's hosting a party tomorrow. Looking forward to it. Will be good to try to feel some sense of normalcy, even if only for a few hours."

After chatting with her mom for several minutes, Madison and her friends departed for the vacation home in Cape Cod—a quaint town named Chatham, roughly a two-hour drive from the airport.

Once in Chatham, they drove down Main Street, towards the house. Chatham was an affluent town on the southeast tip of the Cape, known for its lighthouse, old fishing town charm, and coastal beauty. It was a perfectly sunny day with a few white puffy cumulus clouds dotting the sky. The top of their Jeep Wrangler was off, allowing them to soak up the sunshine and feel the gentle ocean breeze caress their skin. The colder-than-usual April had now turned into a mild May.

As they drove down Main Street, Madison could sense the patriotic spirit, with all the storefronts and restaurants proudly waving American flags. The display was never intended to be an ostentatious show of patriotism but was more about evoking feelings of community and pride in their country. Beautiful flowers lined the streets, including blue, pink, and white hydrangeas—the Cape's signature flower.

After driving past the lighthouse, they went down a few windy roads until finally arriving at Madison's driveway, which was made of crushed seashells. The vacation property was a two-story Cape-style house perched on top of a grassy hill overlooking a large saltwater pond that connected to the ocean. There was even a mid-sized greenhouse in the backyard that contained plenty of fresh fruits and vegetables. The house had the traditional weathered cedar shingles, with a wrap-around porch and second-story balcony along the entire exterior of the house. This provided a perfect view of both the pond below and the homes across the waterway.

All of them jumped out of the Jeep and walked around the property. Madison took them to the large dock that extended out to the pond and showed her friends that in the distance to the left, the ocean and lighthouse were visible. Everyone marveled at the beautiful blue hydrangeas that surrounded the home, providing a burst of color against the grey exterior and white-trimmed windows.

"This house is gorgeous! Why have you not taken us here before?" Bradley exclaimed.

"Yeah, if your mom needs a caretaker to look over the house next summer, please sign me up!" Jessica shouted, already feeling that she could easily get used to the Cape Cod lifestyle.

"How far is Provincetown from here?" Bradley asked. Provincetown was the gay mecca of the east coast.

"Thirty minutes."

"May need to sneak up there one night to find my future husband," Bradley teased.

All of them eventually grabbed their bags in the trunk and after marveling at the gorgeousness of their surroundings, headed inside. They walked into the large open concept entertaining space.

"How inviting. Not a bad place to relax after us nearly getting killed," Bradley said.

Madison smacked his shoulder.

"Hey, you know me. Sometimes the best way to get through a difficult time is to crack a joke. My goal is to pull that smile out of both of you by the end of this weekend."

Madison and Jessica looked at each other and nodded in agreement.

Madison's friends marveled at the large living room, with cream walls and beadboard ceiling. A stone fireplace rose from the left side of the room. The nautical-themed décor included model-sized boats, seashells, and anchors. The ceiling was two stories tall, with expansive windows that extended above the glass sliding doors with views of the water. When the house was updated a few years back, Madison had helped with some of the design.

They proceeded through the living area to the large, updated kitchen and congregated around the kitchen island. She remembered that this was where Mom found Dad in a pool of blood before being rushed to the hospital. This was her first time back to the house after the attack.

"Okay, so keeping in the spirit of trying our best to have some fun, are we going to rush to the bedrooms to pick out the best one, like they do on the *Real Housewives* shows?" Bradley said. He was already eyeing the staircase near the kitchen.

Madison was starting to warm up to the comic relief.

"Well, if we are doing this housewives-style, I get the master suite on the first floor since I'm hosting. I'll let you guys decide how you pick the other bedrooms which are upstairs. There are four bedrooms and three bathrooms so plenty of space."

Jessica took a few more steps forward, trying to sneakily get ahead of Bradley. Madison could sense Bradley understood her intent.

"Okay, it's a race to the best room then!" Bradley shouted.

Bradley tripped over one of the chairs in the kitchen and Jessica pulled ahead, being the first one to get up the staircase near the kitchen. She immediately turned left at the top of the stairs, knowing she wanted a room with a water view. She ended up choosing the largest of the three remaining bedrooms, one with a beautiful view of the pond that opened onto the wrap-around balcony. It also had a private bathroom.

Bradley opened the bedroom next to Jessica, but it was set up as an office with only a small day bed. He walked to another bedroom down the hall—equipped with two twin beds on either side.

"Well, it looks like I'm not going to be hooking up with anyone on this trip," Bradley joked. "I guess I could put the twin beds together and make a king bed."

All three settled into their rooms and unpacked their belongings as Madison did the same on the first-floor master suite. The master suite was where her parents always slept, and this would be one of only a handful of times she stayed there.

Upon entering, a hallway extended on either side. She turned right toward the master bedroom, a large expansive space with cathedral ceilings, and a glass slider that opened onto the wrap-around porch with pond views. The room was airy and bright, much like the rest of the house.

She passed the dresser where various family photos were displayed. One photo of her and her dad caught her eye. It was a photo of them on Chatham Lighthouse Beach when she was about ten years old. As a little girl, he would take her there to look for seashells. In the picture, she proudly held up a large, white seashell to her ear. He used to tell her you could hear the ocean inside.

Madison jumped on the plush king-sized bed to lie down. So comfortable and inviting—home. Her body sank into the bed and it felt as though she was receiving a warm, enveloping hug. Sleep would come easy as she barely got any on the red-eye. She reached for her phone on the bedside table and sent a text to Bradley and Jessica.

Hey guys! Still tired from all that traveling. I think I'm going to take a power nap to recharge. Let me know if you need anything.

Madison laughed at Bradley's reply.

Can't wait to have all the boys over on this twin bed!

Madison closed the door and curtains in the bedroom, played some calming meditation music, and climbed back into bed. After five minutes, she was asleep.

She was right back to the day Dad died. She was seated next to his hospital bed, holding his left hand, and comforting him alongside Mom who was standing to the right, holding his other hand. Everything felt the same as it did that fateful day—she was terrified to lose him. She glanced over to see Mom crying, on the verge of breaking down but trying to stay strong for her daughter.

Dad squeezed her hand, acknowledging that he knew she was there with him. He struggled to lean forward but Madison, still seated, met him halfway as he handed her the gold necklace with a key pendant he was wearing. The same necklace she wore every day since he gave it to her. He whispered something in her ear.

Even in her dream, she could still not understand what he was saying.

"Dad, I can't understand you. Please say it again."

After whispering incoherently once more, he fell back into his bed. Madison and Mom did their best to soothe him.

Suddenly, everything faded, and Madison gently opened her eyes. She felt the same sense of grief as the day Dad passed. All she could do at the moment was cry. Tears flowed down her cheeks. She was crying even harder than when she last dreamed about him.

"Dad, what were you trying to tell me?" Madison called out, hopeful Dad could still hear her.

She wondered why this memory was resurfacing again. The day it happened everything was a blur. After lying down for a few more minutes, she rose from the bed.

She pulled open the curtains in the bedroom, allowing the sunlight to stream in. It was still a glorious day outside. She looked down to see her suitcase and figured it would be best to unpack. She hoisted her suitcase up onto the wide armchair in the bedroom and put all her essential clothing in the dresser.

After pulling out the last piece of clothing from her suitcase, she noticed a small stack of paper tucked in one of the sleeves. She pulled it out and immediately recognized what it was. It was the short story she wrote in middle school, *Whispers*. She must have forgotten to unpack it after arriving back from Connecticut weeks ago. This weekend may be the perfect opportunity to read it again. She set it on the bedside table.

She proceeded to the walk-in closet. This is where Mom's jewelry was stolen the night Dad was attacked. The closet was disheveled that night. Now, it almost looked too perfectly intact. It was unnerving that such destruction could be reversed so quickly.

Physically, things appeared back to normal. Those scars were easy to fix. Mentally, it would never be the same again. Those scars were permanent.

Madison reached for the handle on the top cabinet which was the widest of the stack. The cabinet door opened to reveal a built-in metal safe—it had a tiny keyhole and was locked.

Luckily the set of drawers below it opened. She hesitated, wondering if it was safe to keep her jewelry unlocked, especially after the robbery. Too bad she couldn't open the safe. *Don't be silly, Madison.* Dad's attacker was in jail, and the neighborhood had had no incidents since. She placed her necklaces, bracelets, earrings, and rings in the drawer.

Feeling relieved that she had unpacked, Madison noticed it was 4 p.m. and texted her friends. She could feel her stomach rumble, having not eaten since they stopped for a quick bite to eat on the road.

Hey, you guys up? How do you feel about getting some food and drinks? Let's go in thirty minutes. Just going to shower and get ready quickly! Nothing too fancy.

Within the first few minutes, she received a heart emoji from Jessica.

Madison jumped into the white cast iron clawfoot tub to rinse off. She stared out the large window with views out to the water. Being surrounded by nature brought her a sense of peace. The sunshine streamed through the skylight above.

She eventually threw on a white tank top with white-and-navy-striped shorts. She admired the gold necklace around her neck Dad gave her. She fixed her wavy blonde hair and put on some light makeup—nothing too fancy. She just wanted to feel comfortable. A feeling that she had been missing for too long.

After stepping out of the master, Madison was in the main living area and screamed upstairs.

"All right guys, I'm ready!"

She thought of Bradley's wit. She needed to say something that would get him excited.

"Who needs a cocktail? Let's go!" Madison yelled.

Jessica appeared almost immediately over the second-story railing, wearing a simple fitted T-shirt and short jean shorts. Madison was relieved Jessica also went for the comfortable look.

There was, however, no sign of Bradley.

"Is Bradley with you?"

Jessica shook her head. Madison walked up the stairs.

She proceeded to Bradley's room and found he was under the covers in his bed, unresponsive. She smirked—he had put the two twin beds together. Madison pulled back the covers to find Bradley was fast asleep. She reached forward and shook his whole body.

"Get up! We are heading out for happy hour. You're supposed to be ready!"

Bradley jolted awake. He was shirtless and only in his boxer briefs, still in a daze from having just woken up.

"Crap, what time is it anyway?" he murmured. "I can get ready fast. I'll just throw on some clothes quickly and fix my hair."

He ran to his suitcase and grabbed a pair of short camo shorts, a grey fitted V-neck tee, as well as a pair of sunglasses. After quickly fixing his hair in the bathroom mirror and spraying himself with cologne, he followed the group downstairs.

Madison climbed into the driver's seat of the Jeep as her friends jumped in. After a ten-minute drive, they arrived at Harbor Café, a picturesque seafood shack located directly on the bay. Madison got her favorite—fried clams and French fries. It was lobster rolls for Bradley and Jessica. Comfort food. A large pitcher of beer for the three of them would wash it all down on the warm, sunny evening.

As they waited for their food at one of the picnic tables by the water, Madison raised her glass of beer, with her friends soon following her lead.

"Cheers to the best friends I could ever ask for."

Bradley chimed in, "And cheers to us being survivors."

All three friends clinked their glasses and took a large sip—Bradley nearly chugged his entire first glass.

Madison finally felt she was starting to relax a little.

17

Madison was getting ready for Dawn's pool party and barbeque.

It was 2 p.m. and another perfectly sunny day, even warmer than yesterday when they'd arrived.

Madison, having been to Dawn's social gatherings before, knew it would be an extravagant event, though she also wasn't quite sure what to expect given everything that had happened over the past month. Dawn was still grieving over losing Amy, but she was largely removed from the events that had transpired in San Diego.

Madison texted Dawn earlier in the day.

Hey, excited to see you later. Please let me know if you need me to bring anything. Also, what should I wear?

Dawn responded moments later.

Dress casual. Something patriotic is always nice, since it's Memorial Day. Looking forward to being around friends again. And no need to bring anything. I have everything covered. I'll see you later!

Madison threw on a white and blue paisley print dress, while

Jessica was dressed like she was ready for a patriotic beach party in San Diego, wearing jean shorts, a red-and-white-striped tank top, and a blue bandana with white stars. Bradley initially insisted on only wearing his American Flag speedo—Madison ultimately convinced him to at least put on his white fitted polo shirt and jean shorts over it. He also had a pair of suspenders to complement the outfit.

Though it was a short five-minute drive to Dawn's, they opted to use kayaks to get there as it was situated directly across the pond from Madison's house, within viewing distance. They figured it would be a fun way to show up to the party. And a little exercise would do them good.

After loading two of the kayaks with a few cases of beer and bottles of wine, they embarked across the pond. Luckily the pond was calm, so it was a very easy paddle. At one point, Bradley started rocking the kayak purposely to startle his friends. Madison laughed—thank God for Bradley. As they crossed, music could be heard from the party in the distance.

Five minutes later, they arrived at Dawn's dock, tied up the kayaks, and began unloading the alcohol. Dawn said she didn't need anything, but Madison had felt obligated to bring *something*. They eventually found themselves at a set of wide wooden stairs built into the ground and began to walk up.

Dawn's house was also perched atop a hill overlooking the water—but far more grandiose and estate-like. The house had the traditional weathered cedar shingles, but everything else about it was over the top. The property was in a gated community situated on nearly three acres, almost unheard of for a waterfront property on the Cape. The three-story home had nine bedrooms and twelve bathrooms.

At the top of the stairs, they reached the expansive backyard, which had a gorgeous Olympic-sized saltwater pool, tennis court, and barn stable. The landscaping was always immaculate, with oversized maple trees dotting the property line. There was even a rope swing on one of the trees and a hammock between two others. As a child, Madison had fallen from there a couple of times.

Several guests had already arrived and dotted the property line in clusters. Madison was not surprised by the preppy, rich crowd. Was it the right idea to come to this party? Maybe a relaxing day on the beach would have been better. Too late to turn around now. Madison figured most of these people came from family money in Boston, Connecticut, or New York City. She was accustomed to being around a pretentious crowd growing up, even though her family was not nearly as wealthy. It used to make her feel insignificant and self-conscious. Today she really didn't care. There were more important things to worry about.

Wonder what Bradley and Jessica are thinking right now.

After walking past the pool, Madison eyed the outside bar in front of the guest house, which was staffed with three bartenders and already swarmed by a rush of people eager to order a cocktail. The spirit was lively as the sound of dance music infiltrated the party—people were ready to celebrate a long weekend and have a few drinks.

"What do you guys want to drink?" Jessica asked.

"Let's do a round of tequila shots" Bradley screamed.

Jessica confidently ordered a round of tequila. Madison was happy to see Jessica assume control and take charge of the situation. She was slowly starting to come back to life.

The tequila hit hard. It had a bitter aftertaste, and Madison winced just as she heard a familiar voice scream her name. It was Dawn.

"Madison, I'm so glad you made it! Happy Memorial Day weekend! I missed you."

Dawn then stumbled into Madison and gave her a warm hug, likely already a few drinks in herself.

"So, these are my friends Bradley and Jessica. We all met at Jessica's dance studio. Now Bradley also works at the same company as me."

Dawn pulled Madison aside briefly.

"I know today is all about having fun. I just want to check in to make sure you are doing okay?"

"Thanks. Honestly, it's been the worst year of my life. First losing my dad. Then Amy and my co-workers. We were all attacked. Could it get any worse?"

"I know. I'm so sorry. I can't believe they still haven't caught the killer. Did you confront Zane?"

"It can't be him. He was on a red-eye flight the night of Amy's murder."

"Are you sure it wasn't him? Did he provide any proof?"

Dawn still seemed eager to raise her suspicion of Zane.

"Yes, I saw his itinerary and everything. His social media posts also match his timeline. By the way, please don't post any photos of us today. Don't want anyone to know I'm here. In case it's someone we know."

"Well, they say it's usually someone you're close to." Dawn embraced Madison. "I hope you can get your mind off things today. Maybe even have a little fun. But I understand if it gets too much. Your friends seem nice and I'm glad you guys are so close. Just don't forget about me, okay? You know I always felt a little excluded by you and Amy."

Madison remembered Dawn's angry tirade at the beach before they pranked Zane that one summer. "I hope we can stay in touch more. Amy would have wanted us to be there for each other. It's good to see you again."

"Have a drink…or ten."

Madison shrugged. "Cheers to that!"

They raised their glasses before ordering another round of tequila shots at the bar.

Madison suddenly heard a scream as she set her shot glass down.

She turned to notice that Bradley had jumped into the pool wearing his speedo as the DJ played 'Emotions' by Mariah Carey. He splashed a group of girls who were comfortably enjoying their cocktails in the spring sun. The girls eventually laughed it off as Bradley encouraged them to sing the uplifting melody with him. Making new friends already.

The extravagant party continued into the afternoon. Drinks were flowing and as people became more intoxicated, tight friend groups that had clung together became more free-flowing.

Madison ran into several acquaintances from high school that she hadn't spoken with in years and enjoyed reconnecting and seeing what people were up to. Most of the conversation was lighthearted.

Please don't let anyone bring up the murders.

She found herself at the bar again ordering another round of drinks. She looked to her side and was shocked to see who was standing right next to her.

Kyle? What was he doing here?

Madison had to do a double take. She attempted to look down. *Did he see me?* They locked eyes. Kyle was just as shocked.

"Madison?" He stuttered. "What—what are you doing here?"

Madison rolled her eyes without realizing she was even doing it. She still wasn't sure if she could trust him.

"I could ask you the same thing! What are you doing here?"

"Well…"

Before Kyle could finish a tall girl with jet-black hair approached Kyle and gave him a kiss on the cheek.

Tiffani.

Madison's heart started racing. This had to be a joke. Why were they at the same party as her? They were literally the last two people Madison would want to see on this trip. And why did Tiffani kiss Kyle?

"Oh…hey Madison," Tiffani interjected. "Fancy seeing you here. Happy Memorial Day weekend!"

The fake greeting irritated the hell out of Madison. She knew Tiffani was there to stir up drama. She didn't have time for this. People were dead. A killer was on the loose.

Tiffani continued, "This is some party, huh? So glad my friend Bianca who is friends with Dawn scored Kyle and me an invite. I used to love coming to the Cape in the summers. I'm from Massachusetts originally, you know."

This was new information to Madison, though in all honesty, she didn't care where Tiffani was from. Madison started to sway slightly, already three cocktails and two shots in.

Tiffani and Kyle awkwardly looked at each other.

Tiffani giggled and continued, "So heard Kyle ran into you at the hospital. Not sure if he told you, but we've actually been dating for the past month. He asked me to be his girlfriend the other day."

Tiffani clearly could have also informed her of this news at work. Her giddiness as she spoke started to get to her.

She had to do everything in her power to restrain herself from grabbing Tiffani's hair and dragging her into the pool. The only thing that stopped her is that she knew Tiffani would likely file an assault charge and let everyone at work know. She'd be fired. She couldn't risk that.

"That's adorable," Madison responded sarcastically. She knew she had to cut off the conversation before things got ugly. "Well, I hope you guys have a great rest of your evening. I'm going to go rejoin my friends over there."

Madison tried to pinpoint what irritated her most about the whole situation. She didn't necessarily care that the two were dating. She truly was over Kyle. She was more annoyed over the fact that she instinctively felt Tiffani was dating Kyle to mess with her.

She thought back and remembered there had been a few occasions when he and Tiffani had met at a work party. But this now raised new questions—were they secretly hooking up while Madison and Kyle were still together? Madison was unsure if she wanted to know the answer.

As she walked away, she could hear Tiffani mutter something under her breath. She knew the best way to get under Tiffani's skin was to appear unphased, so she continued to walk confidently toward her friends who were circled around a cocktail table. Bradley was of course still in his speedo.

She knew she was now in for a long night ahead. If she could survive that encounter, she could survive anything.

18

The party continued for several more hours. Drinks flowed, shots were consumed, and guests enjoyed the lavish buffet-style meal that Dawn had organized.

Madison tried her best to enjoy the remainder of the party, but she had sobered up after the run-in with Kyle and Tiffani, which had caught her completely off guard. She avoided them for the remainder of the party.

"We have your back always," Jessica had assured her.

"It's fine. This little drama isn't important in the scheme of things. Our safety is my focus. I love you guys." Madison kissed both her friends on the cheek.

The sun began to set, and guests slowly started to disperse from Dawn's house. Most were planning to attend a bonfire on Chatham Lighthouse Beach. The pond connected to a creek that led directly to the beach. Another opportunity to kayak.

But where was her purse?

Madison looked under several of the pool chairs.

"Hey, Jess. I can't find my purse anywhere. My cell phone is in there too. Can you call it? Maybe we will be able to hear the ring."

Jessica tried calling as Madison walked around the pool area but did not hear it. She had her call again near the bar, which was mostly empty by now, but still no luck. Dawn approached as she sensed her friend was worried.

"Are you looking for something?"

"Yeah, I can't find my purse anywhere. I swear I left it under one of the pool chairs, but it's not there."

"I'm sure it has to be here somewhere. Listen, it's already 8:15 p.m. and I don't want you to miss the bonfire. I plan on skipping out tonight because I need to stay here and do some cleanup. I have a cleanup crew coming tomorrow but some of this stuff needs to get put away tonight. I'll be on the lookout and see if I can find your purse. You go enjoy the bonfire!"

"I feel bad. I wouldn't mind staying back and helping you…"

Madison remembered what Dawn had told her earlier about feeling excluded.

"I don't mind at all! I'm exhausted from socializing anyways and could use some alone time. I'll let you know if I find your purse. I'm sure it will turn up."

She hesitated at first, feeling guilty as she wanted to help Dawn and not leave her alone. After insisting again, she sensed Dawn genuinely wanted her to go.

"You need to have some more time with your friends. Don't let the night slip away. Go. I'm sure I'll find it."

"I'm worried about leaving my phone though."

Bradley continued, "Jess and I have ours. Dawn—give me your number. Text me if you find it."

Madison reluctantly agreed to leave. It would turn up eventually. Certainly, none of the rich party guests needed it.

She and her friends walked down to the dock with the kayaks and hugged Dawn goodbye.

"Thanks for everything, Dawn. We will see you soon."

Dawn waved from the dock as they paddled away. The sun was now below the horizon and darkness was setting in.

CHATHAM, MASSACHUSETTS

Sunday, May 29, 2022
9 p.m.

Dawn proceeded up the wooden stairs past the dock and reached her backyard.

She was glad to have some alone time finally. Though she appreciated being around friends, the recent death of Amy still lingered. She had debated going through with the party at all—now she was exhausted and ready to decompress.

But first came the clean-up. What once was a tastefully decorated party was now in full disarray—plastic cups littered the grass and pool area, along with dirty plates and napkins. Was that vomit on the lounge chair? Decorations were also strewn about and what remained of the American flag cake was smeared on the pool deck.

Someone had apparently tossed it from the dessert table.

Dawn, still a little tipsy from the drinks she had consumed, looked down in disgust and anguish.

She had arranged for a cleaning crew to do most of the heavy lifting tomorrow, but she knew at the very least she would need to refrigerate the remaining food to avoid an onslaught of hungry seagulls in the morning. Her parents were returning in a couple of days—she had to make it look like it was only a small get-together. After grabbing several rolls of aluminum foil from inside, she started wrapping food at the buffet table.

Dawn made several trips from the backyard to the garage with trays of leftover food as there were several industrial-sized fridges and freezers in there. Not your typical garage—it looked like another room in the house, immaculately clean with light flooring, ceiling, and walls. Custom stainless-steel cabinet doors and drawers with harbor blue trim lined the walls, offering plenty of storage. LED lighting brightened up the space further and showcased the cars that were parked, including a Range Rover and Mercedes S-Class sedan. Her dad loved cars.

After thirty minutes of cleaning, Dawn finally loaded the last tray of food in the fridge. As she shut the refrigerator door behind her, she leaned back and stood there to catch her breath. It was a long day and she wanted nothing more than to go to bed. Other than feeling emotionally drained, she had woken up at 6 a.m. to prepare for the party, not to mention that the many drinks she'd had were starting to wear off.

She wondered what her friends were up to. Were they enjoying themselves at the bonfire?

The silence in the garage was soon interrupted by the loud sound of the Range Rover's car alarm going off. The beeping sound reverberated and echoed loudly in the closed garage. She had been driving the car earlier. Maybe she had the keys still in her pocket and accidentally set off the alarm. Nope. They weren't there.

She sprinted toward her car and walked the outer perimeter. Nothing appeared to have triggered it.

Once at the driver's side door, she peered in and noticed the keys were sitting on the seat. Must have left them there after returning from the grocery store. She opened the door, grabbed the keys, and turned off the alarm.

With her body now leaning into the vehicle, she noticed something on the passenger side seat. It was a navy-blue purse that was not hers.

Was it Madison's?

Dawn stepped into the driver's seat, reached for her phone, and called Madison. Suddenly, the navy-blue purse began to vibrate. She opened the gold buckle and pulled out the vibrating phone. Dawn's name appeared.

How did Madison's purse get inside the car? Dawn placed Madison's phone back into the purse and pulled out her own to text Bradley.

Hey Bradley! It was awesome getting to know you today. You really made me laugh, which I desperately needed. Can you give Madison a heads-up that I found her purse in my house? Her cell phone is also in there. She can swing by after the bonfire to pick it up. Thanks babe!

After hitting send, Dawn heard what sounded like a thud from the back trunk. She looked back and saw the trunk door slowly rise until it fully opened.

That was odd.

As she sat in the driver's seat, she reassured herself it was probably nothing. She opened the door and peered to her left toward the back of the car. She couldn't see anyone there. Maybe a party guest had one too many drinks and was pulling a prank on her.

After taking another deep breath, she stepped out and walked slowly to the back of the vehicle. As she turned the corner toward the trunk, anticipating someone was there, she jumped and let out a loud scream hoping to startle them.

The trunk was empty. She laughed at herself for assuming the worst and closed the trunk.

Just as the trunk door closed shut, there was a scraping sound against the garage floor. It sounded like something metal. It grew louder. Dawn realized it was coming from beneath her car. With trepidation, she crouched down to investigate. With her knees now against the floor, she leaned her body down and positioned her head so that she could see what was beneath it.

She squinted and saw someone wearing a gray mask. No mouth. Black pits for eyes. Exactly how Madison described the killer.

A sharp object pierced deep into her left arm. She screamed and accidentally dropped her phone. Blood began to gush from the wound. The person lunged forward again as she quickly rolled on her side—this time the knife barely missed her head. As the killer appeared from under the car, she attempted to grab her phone but couldn't reach it in time. She jumped to her feet and ran. He was in pursuit.

She sprinted toward the tool locker in the garage and began throwing what she could at the killer—wrenches, hammers, and screwdrivers. She had to fight back. One of the wrenches grazed the side of the killer's head, which caused him to stumble backward near the garage door. She opened the door in the garage to the house and locked it.

Dawn leaned up against the door, held the wound on her arm, and realized the cut was deep.

No time. Need to lock the doors in the house.

After running through the mudroom, kitchen, and into the main foyer, she reached the front door. It was now completely dark outside, but she could see the faint glow of the moonlight outside.

As she reached for the lock, the door burst open and the killer lunged at her, knocking her back and causing her to fall to the ground just before the stairs. She was determined not to be overpowered. A struggle ensued before she raised her right leg and kicked the intruder in the groin. The killer cowered over—definitely male. It gave her enough time to push his body off hers and stand up.

With the killer being right in by the front door, Dawn was already up the first few steps to the second floor. The killer got back on his feet and followed her.

At the top of the stairs, Dawn grabbed a large ceramic vase from the landing and tossed it. The vase smashed into multiple pieces against his body, causing him to lose balance and tumble down the stairway to the landing on the first floor.

She wasn't going to go down without a fight.

Dawn raced down the hallway on the right toward the master suite and opened the door to the bedroom. Once inside, she locked the door behind her and looked around trying to determine her next move. She spotted the spiral staircase that led to a loft in the master.

Dawn raced up the staircase and once in the loft, ran to a set of closets on the rear wall. She opened the doors quietly, stepped in, and shut them behind her.

Her heart was racing. Beads of sweat began to appear on her forehead. She counted to herself to see how much time had passed.

Ten seconds.

Thirty seconds.

Ninety seconds.

Don't let him find me.

It felt like an eternity as Dawn counted quietly. The pain in her arm was taking over and she needed to get help fast as she shook in fear.

Please don't let me die tonight.

Suddenly there was a bang on the bedroom door, repeated multiple times. Then came an even louder thud. He must have knocked down the door.

Dawn was able to see out of the closet through small cracks in the plantation-style doors. After several seconds, she saw the masked figure run past the closet, and glance to the left and right before disappearing out of view.

Were those footsteps headed back down the spiral staircase? Dawn clasped her hand over her mouth to keep quiet as the pain in her arm was radiating intensely. She once again counted to herself.

Ten seconds.

Thirty seconds.

Ninety seconds.

She could not hear or see the killer anywhere in her line of sight from the closet. He had to be back downstairs, right? She slowly opened the closet door and still no sign of him.

As she tip-toed out, momentarily breathing a sigh of relief, she suddenly sensed some movement coming from her left. The killer lunged at her. He must have been hiding in a blind spot.

Dawn reacted quickly enough and sprinted toward the spiral staircase. Just before reaching the stairs, he grabbed hold of her hair and yanked her backward. She kicked and screamed as she realized she was now being lifted. Her body was hanging over the top of the banister in the loft.

Dawn fell and landed on the first level of the master bedroom.

Luckily the large king-size bed was directly below. He probably didn't realize she would land there, she thought. The force of the fall was enough to knock the wind out of her for several seconds.

Dawn gasped for breath and finally was able to orient herself. She saw the killer had spotted the crystal chandelier that was hanging directly above the bed. The chandelier was suspended by a long rope and pulley. The rope extended from the chandelier and was fixed to a wall in the loft.

The killer raised the knife and cut through the rope. The crystal chandelier, which had several large sharp glass pieces, came barreling down toward Dawn's head, making a whoosh sound as it went through the pulley. Dawn had little time to react and let out a terrifying scream. A direct impact would undoubtedly cut through her head and kill her instantly.

Just as it seemed certain that the chandelier would impale her, the rope reached the end of the pulley. The chandelier made an abrupt stop directly above her head. She stared up at the thick glass pieces that dangled above, knowing she had narrowly escaped death.

As the killer slammed their hand on the banister, she leapt from the bed and ran out of the master suite. Her pace was rapid, but she was slowly starting to lose energy. She had to find a way out, and fast. She reached the stairway in the main foyer and ran down to the first floor toward the front door.

As she frantically opened it, someone stood in front of her and she let out a scream, as did the other individual.

It was her friend Davina.

"Holy shit, Dawn! You scared the crap out of me! I was just coming by because I left my purse here. Have you seen it by any chance? Um… also are you okay? You look panicked!"

Dawn had a look of terror in her eyes as she stepped outside onto the front porch steps next to her friend, wanting to get out of the house knowing the killer was still inside. She grabbed Davina by the arm.

"We need to get out of here! Amy's killer is in there, and he's trying to kill me too!"

Davina at first thought it had to be a joke. She walked up the stairs and through the front door, then turned back around to face her friend.

"I'm sure it's just someone trying to scare you. Probably one of the party guests making a bad joke or something. I really do need to get my purse. I'm already upset that I missed most of the bonfire."

Davina then finally noticed blood dripping from her friend's arm.

"Oh my gosh. Your arm is bleeding! Is the killer really in there?"

"I was stabbed, Davina! Yes, it's Amy's killer!"

The masked figure appeared behind Davina from the open front door.

"Behind you!" Dawn screamed.

Davina didn't have time to turn around. As she stood near the front door, the knife pierced through her lower back and jutted out through the front of her stomach. She gurgled as blood began to pool from her mouth. Davina looked at Dawn in horror as the killer pulled the knife out and slit her throat.

Davina's body fell to the floor. Dawn stared back at the killer.

"You monster!" she screamed.

Where do I go now? Driveway to the main street is too long. He will outrun me. Need to hide somewhere fast.

She sprinted toward the sideyard as the killer wiped the bloodied knife clean on his black attire. After turning the corner around the garage, Dawn looked behind her and saw he was in pursuit.

She screamed for help.

"Somebody help me! Please…anybody!"

But her cries were soon drowned out by a loud boom. The sky was illuminated with beautiful, bold colors as fireworks started to go off.

Once in the backyard, her feet started to drag along. She was losing steam and starting to feel dizzy. Where to go now? She felt helpless. The killer quickly caught up to her as both neared the pool.

After one last desperate cry for help, Dawn felt his hands clasp around her neck. The killer stabbed her directly in the chest. Immediate pain rushed through her body.

The killer whispered in her ear. Sounded robotic. Not human.

"Killing you will be just as fun as killing Amy."

Before she could respond, she was pushed forward and fell into the pool.

Disoriented, she lifted her head above water and struggled for air. She took several large inhales before feeling the weight of someone pressing her head down into the water. Dawn attempted to fight back but could feel the remaining energy in her body slowly wane away. She saw the water around her turn red. Everything was becoming foggy. Her kicks and punches became less intense.

The last thing she saw was the light from the fireworks in the night sky.

19

Flames licked the charred edges of the wood as a fog slowly rolled in from the ocean.

Couples and small groups stood and said their goodbyes, leaving Madison, Bradley, and Jessica on a blanket beside the bonfire. Madison reached for a sweater. The air was wet now, cold.

"This is relaxing. We needed this." Jessica's tone was upbeat in a strained sort of way.

"I say we don't end the night quite yet," Bradley said. "Let's head back to Madison's for a nightcap. Just us. What do you say?"

Both women nodded. They packed their belongings and walked toward the kayaks. Madison knew it would be good to spend some time alone with just her best friends. Seeing Kyle and Tiffani had thrown things off.

Bradley tapped Madison on her shoulder. "Good news. Dawn found your purse and cell phone at her house. She said you can drop by tonight."

"Awesome. I'll swing by on our way back. You two take the other kayak home. I'll see if she needs help cleaning up. Go ahead and start without me."

"It's a plan. We'll have a shot of tequila waiting for you."

Everyone hugged then jumped into kayaks and paddled away from the beach and down the creek. The fog grew thicker as they reached the inlet. It was cold and eerie. The pond's surface was still and quiet as they made their way through the dark, murky water.

Madison waved. "I'll see you in thirty minutes. Just tie up on the dock, make sure it's secure or Bradley will be swimming for them tomorrow."

"Oh no, I won't."

As Madison's kayak turned toward Dawn's house, she yelled back, "Oh, and pour me that shot. I'll be ready!"

Bradley and Jessica paddled into the distance as she approached Dawn's dock. She tied the line and walked up the wooden staircase and into the backyard. The house and backyard were dark but for the moonlight. Dawn must be sleeping.

Stepping to the right of the pool, she nearly walked into a dark smear on the concrete leading up to the grass line. "Dawn?"

Silence.

"Are you outside?"

No response.

The rear patio doors were ajar and she stepped through them. Strange Dawn didn't close them. "Dawn?" The house was unnervingly quiet and her heart rate quickened. She called out again. Nothing.

No one in the living room or foyer, where the front door hung open a little. She steadied herself, ready to jump back and run. Everything in her said *run now*, but where was Dawn? Was she hiding? She wrapped her fingers around the handle and steadied herself again then pulled the door fast and wide. Nobody there. She turned around. "Dawn, are you asleep? It's Madison. Just wanted to pick up my purse…"

She walked up the staircase to the second floor where a broken vase lay on the wood and wondered if she should go back down to the kitchen and grab a knife. Something. *Breathe Madison. Find a phone.*

The guest bedrooms were untouched but the master suite was a mess; the crystal chandelier pulled down and dangling a foot from the bed, sheets disheveled. No sign of Dawn.

She walked back out to the landing at the top of the stairs and looked through the picture window where the lights from her house glowed across the water. Maybe Dawn was there.

Sitting on the hall table was a pair of binoculars. She picked them up and pressed them to her eyes, panning the property. The fog was still rolling in but had not quite made it to the cottage yet. The yard and wrap-around porch were empty. No one. But framed in the kitchen window, Bradley stood, pouring drinks and dancing. His lips were moving. He must be playing his favorite music, Britney Spears.

The master suite on the first floor was dark but on the second floor, Jessica was drinking a beverage. She stepped out from her bedroom door onto the balcony, turned on the balcony light, and glanced into the distance toward Madison, unaware she was being watched. After a few seconds, Jessica walked back into the bedroom and Madison followed her with the binoculars as she walked into the en-suite bathroom, eventually disappearing. Bradley was still in the kitchen, singing, and dancing. No sign of Dawn.

She laughed a little, watching Bradley dance, and took a deep breath. Time to go home. Dawn must have gone into town. She could get the purse tomorrow.

With one last glance through the binoculars, she intended to capture Bradley's moves to mimic them later—Bradley loved being mimicked—but something distracted her on the balcony. She adjusted the lenses.

It was him.

He was on the balcony moving slowly toward Jessica's door, the same slow step and dark clothes and gray, faceless mask. The same hunting knife. He peered through the doorway and inside Jessica's bedroom.

Jessica emerged from the bathroom shaking her head, unaware. He was standing right there but she couldn't see him. Madison banged on the window in front of her. "Jessica, the killer is outside your balcony door! Run!"

Jessica turned off the bedroom, bathroom, and balcony lights. Crap—no way to see where anyone was now.

Madison frantically searched for a landline upstairs. Nothing. She ran down the stairs to the garage. Maybe Dawn had left her keys in the car. Would be quicker than the kayak. The fluorescent lights above flickered on as she ran to the Range Rover. The door was open but there was no sign of the keys. No time to keep searching.

She turned around and noticed one of the large industrial-sized freezers had blood dripping down the side. Could it be from meat?

She reached for the cover and pulled it up. Dawn's body was covered in ice and surrounded by dead fish. The ice had turned red from all the blood. Her head was protruding. Tiny icicles had formed around the lips, eyelashes, and eyebrows. Her glossy, frozen eyes stared blankly back at Madison as she screamed.

Madison ran out of the garage, through the back patio doors, and past the pool where a long dark figure hung from the rope swing. A lantern sat on one of the tables. She turned it on and stepped toward the swing. It was a body. The woman's long, black hair completely covered her face. There appeared to be multiple stab wounds and gashes to the body. Intestines protruding. Blood everywhere. Red splotches stained her white dress. She pulled back the hair. It was Dawn's friend, Davina. Her face was purple.

Adrenaline pumping, she ran down the wood stairs to the kayak.

CHATHAM, MASSACHUSETTS

Sunday, May 29, 2022
11 p.m.

"We're having fun, Mamá. Been nice to get away for a bit. Madison's cottage is gorgeous. So posh on the Cape, lots of money."

"Just be safe, Mija, okay? I'm glad you are able to relax but I'm worried about you."

"Don't worry. I'll be fine. I have to go now. Friends are waiting. Te quiero mucho, Mamá."

"Te quiero mucho, mi reina."

Jessica hung up and stepped onto the second-floor balcony to look out at the pond in the distance. Fog was continuing to form, though it was still clear in several spots along the waterfront. She could hear

Bradley's dance music playing downstairs. Sounded like Britney.

She stepped back inside to wash her face. She combed her long brown hair that effortlessly flowed down by her side. All this humidity was causing it to frizz. At least a new tan from the day's sun gave her a fresh and youthful glow.

She suddenly heard a loud thud outside the bathroom door.

"Bradley? Madison? Is that you?"

She opened the door and stepped into the bedroom, but there was nobody there. She could only hear the pulsating beats from the music down below. What caused that thud? After turning off all the lights, she walked down the hallway. A nagging feeling that someone was following her caused her to turn toward the dark bedroom again. Still no sign of anyone. The white curtains on the windows billowed from the gentle breeze outside, appearing to effortlessly dance. It looked like a white ghost.

She walked down the stairs toward the kitchen. Bradley was still dancing.

"Bradley, you have to move your hips like this. Also, watch my feet, how they move during this part…"

He tried but was not picking it up.

"All right, Jess, I think it's time for you to have another drink. What are you in the mood for? There's tequila, rum, vodka…pretty much everything actually!"

"You know, I'm kind of in the mood for a tropical drink. I think I'm going to make a mojito. I know we have the rum. I see some soda water and limes on the counter over there. All we need is some mint…" She opened the fridge and looked around but didn't see any mint. "I'm going to check in that greenhouse out back. I'll be back in five."

Jessica walked out the door, stepped onto the grass, and saw the

A-frame modern glass greenhouse on the right side of the backyard.

As she walked, she still felt the nagging feeling that someone was watching her. She turned back toward the house, but no one was following her. Maybe she should go back inside to get Bradley. He was singing loudly now. *Don't want to interrupt his fun. I'll be quick.*

She opened the door to the dark greenhouse and entered slowly, hearing the loud buzz of the fan overhead. Must be running to keep the plants cool. There had to be a light switch somewhere.

Pressing her hand against the wall, she eventually found it, and a fluorescent light flickered on. Countless plants surrounded her, including multiple varieties of flowers, vegetables, and herbs. Each plant was neatly labeled.

Jessica walked down the center aisle, looking on either side of her as she went.

Basil. Spinach. Cilantro. Tomatoes. Strawberries.

Once at the opposite end of the greenhouse, she found exactly what she was looking for—several perfectly manicured mint plants. She grabbed a handful of leaves, her mouth now watering at the thought of the delicious mojito she would soon enjoy.

Well, that was lucky.

After putting them in her pocket, the fluorescent light turned off suddenly. She turned back toward the entrance.

Standing in the doorway was the killer. Gray mask secured to the head with elastic straps. Black pits for eyes. He tilted his head from side to side while staring back at her.

And then he pulled out the knife—black blade with brown leather handle. The moonlight streamed through the glass ceiling, glinting off the blade.

I won't die tonight.

She immediately grabbed several potted plants, hurling them as the killer walked towards her. Several pots made contact but did nothing to deter him.

She turned toward the door behind her and tried to open it. This door was locked—a metal chain secured it.

He was getting closer. After grabbing another potted plant, she threw it at the glass door and the bottom shattered. She got down on her knees and crawled through the opening.

Her hands were in the grass, but the knife stabbed her right foot still inside. The killer grabbed both of her feet and pulled her to him, her body dragging across shards of glass piercing her abdomen and side.

She screamed and kicked his hand as he raised the knife, knocking it away. He placed his knees on top of her legs. She followed his eyeline toward a pitchfork leaning against the doorframe.

He grabbed the pitchfork and held it a foot above her stomach.

"Please, don't kill me!" Jessica begged. "What do you want? I'll do anything."

He stood there as he tilted his head from side to side. He lowered the pitchfork and used the points of it to slowly lift her shirt. The blades felt cold to the touch against her bare stomach. He paused as he got a glimpse of her bra underneath.

The pressure of his knees on her legs relaxed a bit. He appeared distracted. She loosened one leg and kicked as hard as she could. She tried for the groin but only got the inside of his leg, unable to get the momentum she needed.

He lifted the pitchfork in the air and stabbed her in the stomach.

20

Madison jumped out of the kayak and sprinted toward the house.

Britney Spears blasted as Bradley sang. Good sign. At the back porch, she flung open the doors and ran toward the music and Bradley. She threw the speaker against the wall. Britney's voice abruptly cut to silence.

Bradley's face immediately went blank and he put down his drink.

"Dawn's dead! And one of her friends. I found them. Their bodies. He's here! He's upstairs, I saw him through the binoculars, we have to find Jessica, where is she…."

"No. No, Jessica is just outside—"

"Where?"

"She went to look for mint in the greenhouse."

"Where's your phone?"

Bradley looked around. "I don't know. Um—"

"Forget it. We need to find her."

They both sprinted through the open patio door and toward the greenhouse—illuminated not by the greenhouse light but by what appeared to be a firecracker or sparkler.

"Jessica…Jessica…are you here?"

Madison was the first to step inside and let out a scream.

Jessica's body lay on the ground, a pitchfork jutting out of her stomach. Her intestines protruded and blood pooled around her. Even worse, a small firework canister was lodged in her mouth. It was lit setting off sparklers. Jessica's eyes were open, still and wide with fear.

Madison ran outside and threw up on the side of the greenhouse.

Bradley wrapped his arms around her as she wept in horror. Whoever was doing all this, they were becoming even more brutal and vicious. She brushed the tears off her cheeks.

"Where's your phone, Bradley?"

"I left it inside."

"We need to get out of this house and drive to the police station. The killer could still be here, maybe even watching us right now. Follow me so I can get my car keys on the counter inside, grab your phone, and I'll drive us to the police station."

Bradley followed her to the house and insisted on entering first. No movement inside that he could see. They were quiet and walked through the living room to the kitchen. He picked up a fireplace poker along the way, hands trembling as he raised it. Madison saw her car keys in sight on the kitchen counter. He grabbed his phone. They quietly ran to the front door, ready to sprint toward the Jeep.

They opened the front door and found Kyle standing on the porch. Bradley swung the poker at him and Kyle jumped back.

Madison screamed out. "Wait!"

The poker had narrowly missed him.

"You scared the crap out of us!" Madison screamed.

Kyle faced Bradley. "Easy buddy. Put that thing down. Everything okay?"

"No…everything is not okay. Dawn, Davina, and Jessica have been murdered. We're going to the police station. Why are you here?"

"I wanted to apologize for earlier…But wait…did you say Dawn, Davina, and Jessica have been murdered?"

"Yes. I found them. Same killer that's been terrorizing us."

"Let's go. Maybe we should take two cars just in case we need them later." He turned to Bradley. "Do you want to drive Madison's car?"

"That works. Let's get out of here. I'll call the police on the way."

By now, Madison's face was pale and she wasn't speaking. She felt lightheaded. Kyle took her hand and they sprinted to the vehicles in the driveway. Madison handed over her keys.

"There's a police station on Bay Street about five miles away. We'll meet you there, Bradley."

Bradley drove away in the Jeep as Madison stepped into Kyle's Ford Ranger.

They drove for a few minutes.

"My gas is almost on empty. Not sure if we will make it to the police station. This shouldn't take long." Kyle pulled the truck into the gas station. He stepped out and walked to the rear of the truck then he walked back to the driver's side door.

"So apparently this gas station is cash only. Do you have any cash on you?"

"No. I left my purse at Dawn's. I don't even have my phone on me."

"Alright, I'm going to run inside quickly to see if they have an ATM. I'll be right back."

He walked in front of the truck and opened the door to the convenience store. Madison sat in silence for a few seconds, fidgeting nervously with the ring on her index finger. A ring Jessica had given her for her birthday two years ago. The ring accidentally slipped off, fell to the ground, and rolled under her seat. She opened the passenger side door, stepped out, and moved the front seat forward and back. It wasn't there.

She glanced over and noticed Kyle left the car keys on his seat. On the keychain was a mini flashlight. She grabbed it and opened the rear truck door. Using the flashlight, she searched the backseat floor. With the ring still nowhere to be found, she reached her hand far underneath and felt around. She could barely touch the ring and it pushed back behind something. It was large. She pulled it out to get to the ring. It was her missing navy-blue purse. Why was it in Kyle's truck?

She opened it and thankfully her phone was there. She noticed a text message from Aaron, Kyle's nurse co-worker.

Hey Madison—never heard back from you about grabbing that drink. Anyways, I learned yesterday from one of the other nurses that you can do a global search on medication transactions. Most hospitals are using the same automated dispensing medicine cabinet system. Makes it easier for traveling nurses to access. I ran a global search on Kyle. The one I previously ran was just for the machine at Scripps Hospital. Looks like he did a system override for several vials of insulin without an order. From Cape Cod Hospital in January.

The same hospital where Dad passed away. She then spotted a blanket on the back seat and pulled it back. The gray mask. Sitting beside it was the knife—the black blade and worn, leather brown handle was unmistakable.

Kyle was the killer.

And he was now exiting the convenience store, locking eyes with her as he walked toward the truck.

21

Madison slammed the back door of the truck as Kyle stepped out of the building. With keys and phone in hand, she sprinted toward the driver's seat.

"Is everything okay?" he shouted. His pace increased as he got closer. She hopped into the driver's seat and locked the truck as he reached the driver's door.

"Madison, let me in. What's going on here? Looks like you've seen a ghost."

She turned away from the window and started the ignition. He banged on the window. "Open the door now. Madison. Madison!"

He punched the window and she placed her foot on the gas pedal and sped off. Through the rearview mirror she saw him chasing her for a few seconds until he stopped and threw up his hands.

As he disappeared in the rearview, the reality set in. Kyle was the killer. Someone she loved at one point, someone she shared the same bed with at night. *Sleeping with the Enemy.* How could he be such a monster?

She drove and tried to refocus, hoping the truck didn't run out of gas before reaching the police station. At least she was safe now. She knew who it was.

She looked for the Jeep as she pulled into the Chatham Police Station and parked. Thankfully, the Jeep was parked in front. She bolted through the front door and ran to the receptionist sitting behind a glass window, an older woman wearing a blue polo shirt.

"Hi, ma'am, is there something I can help you with?"

"Yes, I need to speak with a police officer right away. Three people have been murdered tonight. My friend Bradley who survived may already be here. The killer is my ex-boyfriend Kyle, and I just escaped in his truck."

The lady behind the glass continued, "Is your name Madison Parker, ma'am?"

"Yes…yes, it is. Assuming you already talked to Bradley?"

"Yes, he arrived fifteen minutes ago and said you would be here soon. He is already being interviewed by two detectives in back. I'll grab an officer to bring you back. One moment please."

"Okay, please hurry. Kyle knows I'm here. He could arrive any minute."

The woman called a cop, who escorted Madison to one of the interview rooms. Upon opening the door, she saw a female detective inside.

"Madison? I'm Detective Leah."

She sat across the table from Leah.

"Bradley told us everything that happened tonight. All about Dawn, Davina, and Jessica. He is in the other room with the other detective. We have multiple police and ambulances responding to the scene. Bradley expressed his opinion that tonight's murders could be connected to other murders in Connecticut and San Diego, so we will be initiating contact with the lead detectives on those investigations as well. Bradley was just telling us that you were on your way with your ex-boyfriend Kyle. We were curious to get a few statements from you to hear your side of the story…"

"Kyle is the killer!" Madison blurted out.

"Wait, what?"

She paused before explaining further.

"While we were on our way here in Kyle's truck, we stopped at a gas station to fill up. When he was inside the convenience store to pay, I found the killer's knife and mask in the backseat. Also my missing purse that was with Dawn before she was murdered. I also have reason to believe he killed my dad."

"What did the knife and mask look like?"

"Knife is some sort of black-bladed hunting knife. Mask is a gray faceless mask. Two eyes with what looks like black filters on them. No mouth. Elastic straps hold it to the head."

"And what's this about your dad?"

"My dad died in January. He was attacked during a robbery and died in the hospital. I always had my suspicions that someone poisoned him in the hospital. Mysterious needle prick in his arm. Kyle had access to hospital medicine as a nurse and I've just found out that he performed a system override for several vials of insulin around that time. He poisoned my dad with it. Possibly as revenge for my dad saying no when Kyle asked for his approval to marry me."

"Where is Kyle now?" Leah questioned.

"I took his truck and drove off. He may be still at the gas station for all I know. Possibly even running this way since he knew I was coming here. He seemed enraged when I took his keys and locked him out of the truck. I've never seen him that angry before—it was like he became a completely different person."

"Can you take me outside to Kyle's truck and show me what you found? We will want to collect it as evidence. I'm assuming you parked in front of the police station?"

Madison nodded. Detective Leah grabbed the male detective in the other room with Bradley, and the three of them walked to the front entrance. Once outside, she led them to the truck and opened the rear door. Part of her feared that the purse, mask, and knife would no longer be there. Maybe Kyle had somehow run to the police station and broken into the vehicle just in time? No one would believe her, and she would end up looking like the crazy one.

But as she opened the door, she saw the mask, knife, and purse still where she'd left them.

She was about to reach for them, but the male detective instructed her to stand back. After taking a few photos of the inside and outside of the truck, he put on a pair of gloves and placed the knife and mask in large plastic bags that were labeled OFFICIAL EVIDENCE.

"The vehicle, along with its contents, will be taken in for further examination and evidence collecting," he declared.

She pointed to her purse.

"Unfortunately, since you claim this was stolen by Kyle, we need to take it in as evidence as well."

Madison shrugged. At least she had her phone on her now.

"Detective Leah will take you back inside to discuss where we go from here. Please don't hesitate to take as much time with her as you need. We are all here to support you and Bradley for what I'm sure has been a very traumatic night."

Leah escorted her back into the same interview room she was in moments before.

"Can I see Bradley now?"

"I'll grab him."

A few minutes later Bradley entered. She hugged him before they both sat down together.

Leah interjected, "Give me a few minutes. I need to coordinate a few things and will be right back. There's some cold water in the mini-fridge under the table, as well as some snacks. Please let me know if I can get you guys anything else." She then walked out of the room.

Madison and Bradley were alone. He leaned over and put his arm around her.

"You think Kyle is capable of this, even killing your dad? I could hear most of it from the other room. I should have never let you drive alone with him. Everything was just happening so fast—I wasn't thinking straight. When he showed up, it didn't even cross my mind it could be him."

"It's not your fault at all. I'm still trying to wrap my mind around Kyle's motivation. Was he that upset over losing me that he felt he needed to kill the people I love?"

"Do you think Kyle acted alone?"

Before she could respond, Leah entered the room again to provide an update.

"Guys, thanks for your patience. Sorry to keep you waiting. I know this has been a long night. First off, I would suggest you reach out to your loved ones if you haven't done so already. I received confirmation from the responding emergency team that they have found the bodies of three individuals at the two residences. We are going to board you both for the night at a motel down the street and assign our best officers, Matt and Josh, to watch guard outside. Rest assured you will be safe under their watch. We did send officers to search for Kyle in the vicinity of the gas station down the road but have so far been unsuccessful in locating him. They will continue to search for a few more hours, but may need to resume in the morning…"

Madison responded, "If Kyle isn't caught tonight, this will never end."

"We will get him, Madison."

If they weren't going to catch the killer, she would.

CHATHAM, MASSACHUSETTS

Monday, May 30, 2022
5 a.m.

Matt and Josh were parked outside the Seaside Motel in the early morning hours of Memorial Day.

Madison was staying in a corner room in the small twelve-room motel and had already fallen asleep. Bradley was a couple of rooms down. Both officers had their windows rolled down so they could hear any potential movement outside. Four hours in, and still no sign of Kyle.

Suddenly, Matt heard a crunching sound coming from the wooded area to the right of the motel. It sounded like footsteps walking through the forest brush.

"You hear that?" Matt asked.

"Yeah, I did," Josh responded.

The crunching sound stopped for a moment, then started up again.

"I'm going to go outside to see what's going on. You wait here to keep an eye on them."

Matt stepped out of the passenger side door of the cruiser and walked in the direction of the woods. With his gun and flashlight drawn, he slowly walked past the motel parking lot, through the grass, and into the wooded area. The fog layer was deepening so he could barely see in front of him. The dead tree limbs and leaves made the same crunching sound he heard moments before. He paused to see if he could hear any other footsteps.

At first, nothing. Just eerie silence.

Then, he heard a loud crunching sound coming from behind him. Matt immediately turned around and pointed his firearm and flashlight in that direction. All he saw were trees and bushes.

He pointed the flashlight toward the ground and saw the outline of bootprints in the dirt—they weren't his. With gun drawn, he followed the trail. They continued for several feet, abruptly stopping at the base of a tree. There were several wooden ladder steps nailed to the tree, ascending the trunk. Matt saw boot scuffs on a few of the ladder rungs.

As Matt shined his flashlight up the base of the tree, he saw a shiny metal object swing in his direction. He briefly felt the blade of an ax pierce the left side of his neck and out the right side.

Matt's head rolled on the forest floor as his headless corpse fell to the ground, blood spattering the surroundings.

* * *

Josh was still sitting in the police cruiser, waiting for Matt to return. Early morning radio was playing George Michael's 'Careless Whisper'. He was reading a magazine, eating trail mix, and quietly humming to the riff of the saxophone. What was that sound outside? A thud followed by what sounded like a bowling ball rolling on the forest floor?

A few minutes later, the passenger side door opened. Still looking down at the magazine, Josh responded.

"Nice of you to finally return, buddy! Find anything in those woods other than a bunny or two?"

When there was no reply, Josh lowered his magazine and looked to his right. It wasn't Matt. It was someone wearing a gray mask and dressed in all black.

The killer raised the knife and stabbed Josh directly in the throat. Josh gagged on his own blood as it poured from his mouth. While trying to desperately reach for the gun in his holster, the killer raised the knife once more and stabbed the officer directly in the eye and through his skull. He retracted the knife and Josh's eyeball came out with it, landing on the dashboard as it oozed fluid.

His body, still seated, fell to the side against the door as the killer wiped the knife blade clean. The haunting alto sax melody of 'Careless Whisper' slowly faded.

22

Madison was at the hospital. Dad was there. Something felt different.

There was a book next to his hospital bed. It was her short story, *Whispers*. She picked it up and read the title aloud.

Whispers

Whisper

She felt the warmth of his hand as she held it. Dad whispered something as he handed her a gold key pendant necklace he was wearing.

His whisper was inaudible. She leaned in closer.

And closer.

The whisper became more audible. She could hear Dad's voice as he continued to point to the necklace.

The safe.

Madison opened her eyes and awoke in the motel. She grabbed for the gold necklace around her neck. Something outside had woken her up. It had sounded like a moan. She reached for her phone on the bedside table, jumped out of bed, and pulled back the curtain. Through the fog, she saw the faint outline of Josh in the police cruiser. Looked like he was asleep. Phew.

She looked down at the door and noticed a piece of white paper under her door. She reached down and unfolded it. Same handwriting as the other note.

> HOT TUB. YEARBOOK. FISH. SPARKLER.
> DON'T YOU GET IT?

Zane. He was in on it too, along with Kyle. Two killers. Amy was killed in a hot tub. Amy, Jared, and Kristin's yearbook photos were planted for her to find after they were murdered. She found Dawn's body in a meat freezer, surrounded by dead fish. Jessica had a Fourth of July sparkler set off in her mouth. *The prank.* Zane was forced to kiss a dead fish, naked and humiliated in the hot tub, on the Fourth of July after he professed his love for Amy in her high school yearbook.

She threw on a pair of jeans and a white tank top, grabbed the Jeep keys, and ran out the front door to the police car screaming Josh's name. He was hunched over and still. She opened the door and his body fell to the ground. Blood was everywhere. He had a huge hole in his throat. One of his eyes was missing.

"Matt!" she screamed. No sign of him anywhere. He was likely dead too. The two best officers that were supposed to protect her were now dead. She reached for the microphone on the police car radio.

"Officers down. Please send help! Seaside Motel in Chatham!"

No time to wait for more police to arrive. She had to take matters into her own hands. She grabbed the pistol out of Josh's holster. Glock 22. Her, Zane, and Dad had gone to the shooting range a few times before Zane was deployed.

Where could she find Kyle and Zane? The Cape house. Where the prank occurred the summer before college. Should she wake up Bradley in his room? No—she didn't want to put him in danger. This was her battle to fight. She opened the door to the Jeep and sped toward the Cape house. No looking back now.

Once there, she parked on the curb and saw yellow police tape surrounding the property. The ambulance, police cars, and crime scene investigators from earlier were now gone. They must have left just hours before, and would likely return later that morning. She ducked below the yellow tape and unlocked the front door. After turning on the lights inside, she cautiously entered each room, gun drawn.

Adrenaline was pumping. Her heart was racing. The family room and kitchen were clear. She turned on the lights in the master bedroom and bathroom. Nothing. She opened the door to the master closet. She pushed aside some of the clothes to see if anyone was hiding behind them. That's when she spotted the cabinet with the metal safe.

Dad whispered *the safe* in her dream. For months, she had desperately been trying to figure out what he had whispered to her that day. There must be something in there he wanted her to find. She opened the cabinet door to reveal the metal safe. Tiny keyhole.

She'd had the key all along.

She unclasped the gold key pendant necklace from around her neck, placed the key in the keyhole and turned it slowly. The safe door opened. A few pieces of jewelry. Several rolls of cash. And a stack of papers.

She took the stack of papers out and placed them on the center island in the closet, along with the gun. Several printed emails.

One was recent, from December 2021. The subject was *Will*

Amendment and was addressed to Dad's attorney, Cliff.

> *Dear Cliff,*
> *I would like to draft up an amendment to my will. Specifically, I would like to change the beneficiaries. My wife is to get half of my estate, whereas my daughter Madison is to get the other half. Please remove Zane as a beneficiary. Everything else can remain as is.*
>
> *Please fax a copy for me to sign to my number at Cape Cod as I am here through the New Year.*
> *Sincerely,*
> *William Parker*

The next page was a response from Cliff that same day.

> *Dear William,*
> *We will amend the will and fax you over a copy to sign. Please note this will isn't considered valid until fully executed and signed by a witness.*
> *Sincerely,*
> *Cliff*

Dad must have felt betrayed by Zane and wanted him out of the will. He couldn't trust him with money. The embezzlement scheme was likely the final straw. At the back of the folder was a final stack of papers held together by a paperclip. She immediately realized it was a copy of her father's will amendment and flipped to where the beneficiaries were listed. Jane and Madison were primary beneficiaries. Zane had been removed completely.

The will amendment was signed by Dad and Amy's stepfather,

Alexander, a witness, on January 2, 2022, days before he was rushed to the hospital after the robbery. If it was signed, how was Zane still getting a portion of the estate? She remembered Mom mentioning that Dad was working on an amendment, but they were never able to locate the signed copy. It was possible that Dad wanted Madison to make the discovery knowing he would likely die in the hospital. Starting with the key he had gifted her.

She put the stack of paper back in the folder and stood there for several seconds trying to piece together the tragedies over the past several months. She felt like she was missing a piece of the puzzle.

Madison walked back to the safe to see if there was anything else inside. Just a custom photo book from Zane's time in the Army. Dad must have gifted it to him and made a copy for himself. The front photo was of Zane standing in front of an American flag, dressed in his Army uniform. Madison flipped through—another photo of the family and Zane outside a military aircraft the day he was deployed to Iraq. Mom and Dad were nervous about him going. The next photo was of Zane saluting the American flag. Various photos of Army vehicles and tanks.

There were several from his deployment. Zane with a group of soldiers dressed for battle. Carrying a large gun and wearing a bulletproof vest, thick pants, knee pads, and boots. She recognized something else. A mask. It appeared hard—must be bulletproof. It was gray with elastic straps that secured it to his head. Faceless with black pits for eyes. Was that a brown leather handle of a knife protruding from his leg holster? Not a hunting knife, a combat knife.

As she peered closer, she suddenly heard a floorboard creak behind her.

Someone leaned over and whispered in her ear.

Hello, Madison.

Before she could grab the gun, she felt a large object hit her over the head. Then everything went dark.

23

Hazy and dark. A pain seared at her temple as Madison slowly opened her eyes. She tried to pull her hand up to her head but two pieces of rope held her wrists to the chair beneath her. Ankles too.

A faint light was coming through the basement window and hitting the random family throwaways Mom had relegated through years of summers and vacations. Boxes of family photos, forgotten Fourth of July sparklers, flower arrangements. She would never use them again but she was always bad at clearing the trash. This was her island of forgotten things.

It was still foggy outside. A robin was sitting upon the window frame. It bent its head down as if it could see her, bleeding and tied to this dirty, basement chair. Funny, Mom bought the chair at a lawn sale when Madison was thirteen, that perfect summer. It had been valuable once. And she vowed to have it recovered and reappointed, but like most things in the family, it fell off in the mind and settled into the recesses.

The robin flitted its wings, rose a little from its perch, then settled again, beginning a sweet song, light and trill.

Two wide, dark streams of what could only be blood lay against the white of her tank top. Fuck. Fuck. Fuck. Her temple throbbed. Had to get out. She could fit through the window. She'd done it years ago, but the ropes wouldn't give. They rubbed at the raw spots on her wrists and ankles. Blood started to pool in the threads.

Footsteps above. Slow and wandering then intentional, heavy like a man's. Two distinct sets. When the basement door opened, the air seemed to siphon itself out. She held her breath as Kyle slowly stepped down onto the landing, turned the corner and came into the basement. His mouth was taped with duct tape, and his hands bound with rope. He had several abrasions on his arms and forehead where sweat dripped down onto his cheeks and neck. He wore the same T-shirt and jeans as last night when he drove her…tried to drive her to the station.

Behind him appeared the man in all black, the same gray, faceless mask, carrying the long knife. He pushed Kyle to the corner of the room and set the knife on the basement floor beside him. He roughly tied Kyle's hands and feet and tied him to a set of pipes. He then picked up the knife and stood, staring down at his captive, turning the knife slowly in his hand, working it all out.

"What do you want from us?" Madison screamed.

"You know what I want."

She caught her breath. It made sense. And if she were honest, some part of her knew it was just him all along. He pulled the mask from his face. He had cuts and scrapes on his cheeks and forehead, his dark hair slicked back with sweat. Her brother's features were more prominent than ever, as if he'd chiseled himself onto his own form. But wasn't that what he had been doing? Making himself complete. He was entirely himself now.

"Zane—you don't have to do to this."

"Don't act like you care. Pretending. You were always good at that. A great pretender."

"It was never pretend." She glanced at Kyle struggling to loosen his ties. "You need help. This isn't you. Let me help you—"

"I loved you most, you know. You were daddy's girl. Family favorite. Best grades. Best schools. Dream job. Big promotions. Everyone loved and adored you. But I loved you most. It was always me."

"I know. I'm sorry. I should have spent more time…"

"Don't lie to me."

"I'm not. I love you. You're my brother. We were there for each other growing up and drifted apart as we got older. I didn't mean to ignore you. Things just got—"

"Busy?" He was turning the knife in his hand again. "You always got it easy. After you were born, everything changed. You took my childhood away from me. You took love away from me. You took everything away from me! It's finally your turn to have something taken away from you."

"You didn't have to kill over sibling jealousy."

"Call it sibling payback. I tried to forget when you hurt me the summer before you went off to college. But do you realize how much you, Amy, and Dawn humiliated me? Rejection isn't fun Madison. It can make you do crazy things."

"How did you kill Amy? You were on a red-eye flight then."

"Snowstorm, remember? The original flight was canceled, and I was rebooked on an earlier flight."

"Was that really why you did all this? Because of a prank we played on you when we were younger?"

"To you, it was just a prank. A game. So I came up with a game of my own. The clues I left were a bonus."

"If I knew I was going to hurt you that bad, I would have never done it. I felt extremely guilty and you know that."

She was fuming with anger inside but had to play nice. He was still holding the knife.

"Well, it wasn't the only reason. You read Dad's will. He was going to cut me out of it completely. I found one of the signed copies on the kitchen counter at the Cape house when I visited in January. Dad was getting ready to send it to his attorney. Wish I knew there was another copy in the safe. I confronted Dad about it and he was still irate over the embezzlement thing. We got into a fight and I hurt him. Bad. Staged the whole thing as a robbery—even gave Mom's jewelry to the homeless drifter to frame him for the crime. Once I found out he was still alive at the hospital, I injected him with a needle while you were gone with Mom—insulin. Knew it wouldn't come up in a toxicology test. Nice try, Madison."

"But, Kyle—"

"Not hard to get someone's fingerprints. They're everywhere. A phone screen. A soda can. All you need for a synthetic fingerprint is acetate paper, a laser printer, and wood glue. Simple hack into an automated medicine machine. And planting evidence in someone's car is pretty easy too. Remember my buddy who was killed in Iraq? I still had his combat knife and mask too."

Madison was sobbing. "How could you kill Dad over money?"

"Well, honestly I killed him for disowning his only son. He wanted to give more of a share to you. His darling Madison. I trusted you. You were one of the few people there for me growing up. Then you decided to make a mockery of me with your friends. I tried to let that go. But the will was the final straw. It felt like yet another betrayal. Another rejection."

"I didn't even know anything about his will. It's not fair to blame me."

"Always pretending like you care. If you cared, you would know what's really going on in my life. I lost my job a year ago, Madison. There's no sales job. I'm a failure."

Madison was still struggling with the ropes around her wrist. She could not break free.

"I can help you. You're going to need someone to vouch for you when this all comes out. You could still be suffering PTSD from your deployment." She had to think of a way to stall him. He was getting more agitated.

"I won't need help. You already told the cops who the killer is. Our buddy Kyle over here, the killer nurse who went on a murderous rampage to seek revenge for his girlfriend wanting to end things. And guess who saves the day and kills him in self-defense? Me. There's no better story than an Army veteran who stopped a serial killer on Memorial Day."

Zane slowly started walking toward the corner of the room where Kyle was tied up. He brandished the large knife in his hand, the black blade gleaming. As he got closer, Madison saw another person appear near the stairwell. It was too dark to see who it was. She could only see a shadow. They were holding a large object—it looked like a baseball bat. Zane heard footsteps behind him, but it was too late.

The metal bat contacted the back of his head, knocking him to the ground. The person raised the bat once more and swung at Zane a second time, this time hitting his back as he lay on the ground.

"Don't even think about laying a hand on my boyfriend!" the woman holding the bat screamed. Madison recognized Tiffani's voice immediately.

"Tiffani, how—"

"Well, when Kyle didn't come back to the hotel last night, I was worried. He said he was driving here to apologize for the altercation between us at the party."

"We will explain everything later. Untie us first. We need to get a hold of the police right away," Madison responded.

Tiffani began untying the ropes around Madison first.

"I appreciate you coming to the rescue. Wasn't expecting that."

"I can put the petty drama aside." She gave a slight smile. It looked genuine this time. Tiffani freed both of her hands. As she was untying her feet, a dark figure approached from behind.

"Behind you!" Madison screamed.

Tiffani fell to the ground after suffering a blow to the head from the baseball bat.

"Maybe we'll just go ahead and kill you first, Madison." Zane sneered.

Zane dropped the bat and flaunted the knife once more. "If you don't fight back, it will be over sooner."

He raised the knife in the air. Madison finally freed her right foot from the chair thanks to Tiffani loosening it for her. She raised her leg and kicked Zane in the groin, knocking herself backward in the chair. The wooden chair legs cracked against the cement floor and she was able to free her left leg. Zane tried to stab her again. He missed. The knife lodged in the wooden chair. He put his hands around her neck and squeezed as she gasped for air. His grin radiated pure evil.

She frantically began scouring the ground with her right hand.

Eventually, it landed on the handle of the knife wedged in the chair. Zane didn't see that she dislodged it.

"Send Dad my regards, Madison!"

Madison raised her right hand and stabbed Zane in the chest. It cut deep, through his back. Blood splattered onto her chest and face. He gurgled on his own blood before collapsing to the floor.

She limped over to the corner and untied Kyle. Both locked eyes and embraced, thankful the nightmare was finally over.

24

Red and blue lights lit up the neighborhood again. Several ambulances and police cars were lined up around Madison's house. Neighbors watched from their homes as the normally quiet street roared with activity.

Madison was sitting on the front porch with Bradley—he had just arrived.

"Can't believe you snuck out of the motel and didn't grab me first!"

"Didn't want you to get hurt."

"Well, hey, if it weren't for you coming here, they may have never caught Zane. You're one bad ass chica."

Jessica always called her that.

Madison sat down with two police officers to talk. Two paramedics were wheeling Zane out on a stretcher. An oxygen mask was around his face. He was barely alive.

She also saw Kyle inside an ambulance in the driveway comforting Tiffani. Her head was wrapped with several bandages but she was still alert. Kyle kissed her on the forehead as the ambulance doors closed and drove away.

While Madison was talking with the officers, she saw her mom pull into the driveway. Mom ran toward her, with Penelope following close behind. They hugged for what seemed like an eternity. Tears streamed down both of their faces. Madison felt the gentle pawing of Penelope at her feet and reached down to pick her up, giving her several kisses.

She was relieved to see Mom, but terrified to break the news to her about Zane. Their family would never be the same.

She may be related to Zane by blood. But he was no longer family.

25

Diffused light brightened the sky. Sunrise was approaching. Madison sat on Chatham Lighthouse Beach with a pen and paper in hand. She drew the sweatshirt tight around her. Summer was only a week away. She was listening to Celine Dion's 'A New Day Has Come'. She and Amy loved Celine. They used to sing her songs in front of the mirror while getting ready.

She followed every lyric of the song as she let out a large exhale. The symbiotic relationship between opposites.

Mom and Bradley were back at the Cape house. They agreed they would make breakfast. They drove up yesterday morning to organize the house since the investigation had finally wrapped up. Mom was still devastated. She was debating selling the house. Zane was no longer in critical condition and was awaiting trial.

Madison yawned. She and Bradley were up late last night entering a dance competition in San Diego in Jessica's honor. They still had a few months to practice.

A copy of the short story she wrote in eighth grade, *Whispers,* sat beside her on the beach towel. Mom found it at the house and read it. Mom loved how the woman in the story was brought back to life after it was discovered that she was murdered. Resurrection. She encouraged her to turn it into a novel and publish it one day. Madison initially dismissed the idea but now here she was planning it out in her notebook. Today would be the start of breathing new life into the story.

She thought of Amy who would always offer her encouragement, like the time she told her to audition for the high school musical. She thought of Jessica who inspired her to pick up dance again.

The sun's upper limb broke the horizon. Sunrise. The sky illuminated like a rainbow—red turned orange, then yellow, and finally blue. She grabbed hold of the gold necklace around her neck that Dad gave her. A seagull flew effortlessly along the top of the water.

Three seals broke the surface and followed each other as they continued to jump.

She remembered Coronado Beach with Dad at sunset. And what he whispered.

Think back to what excited you as a kid. Don't let that dream die.

She could feel Dad's presence.

She felt more awake than ever.

Spring had never felt so alive.

ACKNOWLEDGMENTS

Some of my most treasured memories are growing up in the '90s where life seemed a lot simpler. I had a particular love for slasher films which I was far too young to be watching at the time. I remember stealing my older sister's VHS tapes of *Scream* and *I Know What You Did Last Summer* so I could watch them with my friends. The opening scene in *Scream* with Drew Barrymore still haunts me. I thank all the slasher fans that enjoyed the thrill of watching these movies growing up—so much so that we still talk about them today. I hope I was able to re-create that experience for you with *Whisper*.

Writing this book was also very personal for me and helped me cope with the grief of losing my dad to Parkinson's disease in 2020. I remember watching old TV re-runs of the *Halloween* movies with my dad even though my mom would have flipped out if she knew. My dad had a huge passion for collecting books, particularly horror and sci-fi, which I didn't quite understand at the time, but I do now. After he passed, while sorting through boxes in my parents' basement, I found a short story I wrote as a pre-teen that was the catalyst for writing

Whisper. I thank my dad for leading me to find it and for helping me to rediscover my passion for writing. Each one of us had "our thing" we loved as kids, and I hope all my readers can reclaim that joy as adults.

Thank you to everyone who gave their time and talent to support this book, including my wonderful editors and designers.

Thank you to my family and friends for cheering me on and taking the time to provide feedback before the book's release. I would like to especially thank my beta readers Jen Visconti, Amber Baldridge, and Miranda Haas. Your strength and resilience are inspiration for the female characters in my book.

Finally, to my readers—I thank each one of you for taking this journey with me. You are the reason this book exists. If you enjoyed this book, a positive review would mean the world to me. Like other debut authors, I rely heavily on recommendations to reach new readers. I hope this book is just the start of our journey together. I can't wait for what the future holds.

ABOUT THE AUTHOR

Brian Dearborn lives in San Diego, California. When he's not busy listening to '80s and '90s songs, he enjoys playing with his beagle, Lucky, and French bulldog, Tinsley. *Whisper* is his first novel.

CONNECT ONLINE:

◉: @briandearborn

𝕗: @briandearbornauthor

♪: @therealbriandearborn

Manufactured by Amazon.ca
Acheson, AB

13378533R00143